THE ILLUSTRATED

SHERLOCK HOLMES

SIR ARTHUR CONAN DOYLE

Adapted by
Nigel Flynn and Richard Widdows

This edition published 1993 in the United Kingdom by MMB,
an imprint of Multimedia Books Limited,
32 - 34 Gordon House Road, London NW5 1LP

Editors: Nigel Flynn and Richard Widdows
Design: Janette Place
Jacket design: Peter Bennett
Production: Hugh Allan

A catalogue record for this book is available
from The British Library

ISBN 1-85375-131-6

Printed in the Czech Republic by Imago

CONTENTS

Arthur Conan Doyle and the World of Sherlock Holmes

Edinburgh in the mid 1850s was a squalid place. The "Old Town" was a maze of tenements and poor houses, its gutters littered with garbage. Disease was rife and murder common — mostly by strangling and knifing. It was here that, on May 22, 1859, Arthur Conan Doyle was born. He was to become famous for creating two of the best-known characters in popular English literature, Sherlock Holmes and Dr Watson.

Arthur's early years with his parents were spent moving restlessly from house to house, in search of a haven from the pollution and grime of the old city. Amidst genteel poverty, Mary, his mother, would tell him stories of medieval honour and romance and of knights in shining armour. Arthur's vivid imagination was stirred by these tales, and by visits to London, whose backstreets matched those of Edinburgh; he was particularly drawn to Madame Tussaud's waxworks and the Chamber of Horrors. Like Sherlock Holmes himself, Conan Doyle was to become increasingly excited by murder cases throughout his life.

Arthur's schooldays were hard. He was sent to Stonyhurst, a strict Jesuit school where, as he recounted later, "they tried to rule too much by fear — too little by love or reason." From Stonyhurst, he went to Edinburgh University to study medicine, in 1877. Here he met Dr Joseph Bell, who was to provide the model for Sherlock Holmes. Dr Bell was an authority on criminal psychology and a man with a taste for the art of deduction; it was "detail" he taught his students to observe.

Always an avid reader, Arthur devoured works of science, theology, spiritualism, mysticism and metaphysics, and he also began to write — two of his short stories were published while he was still at university. His taste for adventure was also very strong; before leaving Edinburgh, he sailed as ship's surgeon on board the *Hope* to the Arctic.

After graduating from university, Conan Doyle established his first practice in Portsmouth. Then in 1885 he married Louise Hawkins, the sister of one of his patients. Happy for the first time in his life, Conan Doyle devoted his leisure hours to the art of the detective story.

Inspired by the writings of the American author Edgar Allan Poe, and the French detective-story writer Emile Gaboriau, he developed his sense for the macabre and his passion for detail to the full. Like Gaboriau, he told his stories through a narrator. This was to be Dr John Watson, who took on many of the characteristics of Conan Doyle himself. Like Conan Doyle, Dr Watson is kindly, sensible and composed; he enjoys sea stories and sport, is courageous and tends to be a romantic. He is loyal and self-effacing, yet capable of being headstrong and perhaps a little too rash at times.

Sherlock Holmes began life as "Sherringford Hope", but changed when Conan Doyle took inspiration from the names of those around him. "Sherlock" was the name of a locally admired cricketer, and "Holmes", the name of a pioneering investigator into the workings of the criminal mind. Thus, "Sherlock Holmes" was born. He and Dr Watson in many ways reflected the opposing sides of their creator's own personality. Holmes is descended from a family of squires, has grey eyes, a brilliant brother, and suffers from alternating moods of elation and depression. He can be impatient and sharp and has a bizarre sense of humour. He is familiar with an extraordinary range of subjects and is at heart a solitary man. He has an almost uncanny grasp of events, a talent which no doubt sprang from Conan Doyle's strong interest in the supernatural. Similarities between the author and his creation also extend to their places of address: Holmes' first rooms were in Montague Street, London; Conan Doyle lived in Montague Place.

In December 1887, Beeton's Christmas Annual published the first Sherlock Holmes story, *A Study in Scarlet*. Interest in the story was heightened by the notorious Jack the Ripper murder cases. The public responded well to the story, which was shortly followed by a second, *The Sign of Four*.

In the summer of 1890 a new popular picture magazine, *The Strand* was launched, and the editor was ecstatic about the Holmes stories — calling Conan Doyle "the greatest short-story writer since Edgar Allan Poe". He wanted one Holmes story a month! So Conan Doyle abandoned his medical practice and devoted all his time to writing.

Yet Conan Doyle was never completely happy with the success of his famous sleuth. He felt that Holmes overshadowed his other writings, but growing popular demand and encouragement from his mother ensured Holmes' survival until 1893, when the famous detective met his death by plunging over the Reichenbach Falls in *The Final Problem*.

The public mourning and outrage which followed Holmes' "death" took Conan Doyle completely by surprise. He was suffering increasingly from insomnia and nightmares made worse by the shock of his father's death and also from the discovery that his wife had tuberculosis — and he became deeply involved in spiritualism. The horror stories he wrote became even more grisly and macabre. However the public were clamouring for the return of Sherlock Holmes, so Conan Doyle engineered his comeback in a story centred around the legend of a huge, terrifying hound — *The Hound of the Baskervilles*. This was to become the most popular of all the Holmes stories. The resurrected Holmes had fresh characteristics: he mixes in much higher social circles than before, and his opinions are sought by the rich and famous.

In July 1906 Louise Conan Doyle died, and her devoted and loyal husband was devastated. The author lapsed into a deep depression and became quite ill. Nevertheless, he remarried a year later, resumed his writing, and his working day became as gruelling as ever — often lasting from dawn through to the early hours of the morning. In his final years he was one of the richest writers of his age, and also completely obsessed with spiritualism. He died on July 7, 1930 though many of his admirers claimed they received spirit messages from him long after his earthly remains had been laid to rest.

Sir Arthur Conan Doyle surrounded by his most famous characters, as drawn by Sidney Paget. Portrait by Henry L. Gates courtesy of The National Portrait Gallery; drawing reproduced by kind permission of Westminster City Libraries, Marylebone.

A Study in Scarlet

Introduction

A Study in Scarlet was first published in *Beeton's Christmas Annual* in December 1887. This small paperback was priced at one shilling and showed on the front cover the picture of a man reaching up from his desk to light an oil lamp. That man was Sherlock Holmes, the world's first and only consulting detective.

The story was a great success. "The author shows genius," declared *The Scotsman*, "he has . . . shown that the true detective should work by observation and deduction." The *Bristol Mercury* summed up simply what millions of readers were to feel worldwide: "The story is very exciting and well told."

An exciting story, well told. This is what Arthur Conan Doyle had tried to do. He introduced to his readers a powerfully intelligent character who, though not a professional detective, nevertheless is able to solve a difficult and intriguing murder case simply by "observation and deduction". Holmes never tires of telling his companion, Dr John Watson, that these two great abilities are all the true detective needs in order to solve crimes. Inspectors Gregson and Lestrade, the Scotland Yard detectives, fail because they always seem to jump to (the wrong) conclusion. By looking carefully and thinking clearly, Sherlock Holmes is able to build up a picture of exactly what happens, piece by piece.

In his quest for the truth, Holmes does not confine himself to a rigid set of methods, but is helped by those whom the police would never have thought of asking — a gang of small boys who, having nothing better to do with their time, stand around street corners and watch everything that goes on around them. Unrestricted by a busy daily routine, they see much more than most people. So naturally a shrewd observer like Holmes uses them to help him unravel the mystery.

In the end — but that would be giving it away — the reader has been taken on a journey of mystery, murder and adventure that has spanned two continents and many years. Patiently, slowly, Holmes works it all out, much to the amazement and admiration of the murderer.

At the beginning of the story, Holmes says: "There's the scarlet thread of murder running through this episode: a study in scarlet, one might say. And our duty is to unravel it, and expose every inch of it." How Holmes does his duty is told in this, his first important case.

1 The Lauriston Gardens Mystery

It was on 4 March 1881, as I have good reason to remember, that I rose somewhat earlier than usual and found Sherlock Holmes, having finished breakfast, pacing the room in a restless mood.

"What's the use of having brains in our profession," he demanded, "when there is no real crime these days? There is not a man alive, nor has ever lived, who has brought the same amount of study and of natural talent to the detection of crime, as I have done. But what is the point, when there are no real crimes to solve or real criminals to detect?"

Annoyed at such arrogance so early in the morning, I thought it best to try and change the topic of conversation. Looking out of the window, I happened to see a smartly dressed man walking slowly down the opposite side of the street, looking anxiously at the door numbers. In his hand he held a large envelope, and was evidently the bearer of a message.

"I wonder what that fellow is looking for?" I asked casually.

"You mean the retired sergeant of Marines?" replied Sherlock Holmes.

"How on earth do you know that?"

But before Holmes could answer, there was a loud knock on the front door. "See what he

wants, will you Watson? There's a good chap."

Keen to discover whether the man really was an ex-sergeant of Marines, and if so, what business he had with us, I went down to the front door. On opening it, the fellow thrust the envelope into my hand and said, "For Sherlock Holmes."

"May I ask what your trade may be?"

"Commissionaire, sir," he said gruffly. "Uniform away for repairs."

"And were you ever at the colours," I asked.

"A sergeant, sir, Royal Marines. Old army man yourself, sir?"

"Briefly, yes. Thank you. Good day to you."

The man clicked his heels together, raised his hand in salute, and was gone.

"How in the world did you deduce that?" I asked Sherlock Holmes after handing him the letter.

"Deduce what?"

"Why, that the messenger was a retired sergeant of Marines."

"I have no time for trifles," he answered curtly. Then with a smile he said, "Excuse my rudeness. You broke the train of my thoughts. So you actually weren't able to see that the man was an ex-sergeant of Marines?"

"No, indeed. Was it that obvious?"

"It was easier to know it than to explain *how* I know it. If you were asked to prove that two and two make four, you might have some difficulty. And yet you are quite sure of the

fact. Similarly with this fellow. Even across the street I could see a great blue anchor tattooed on the back of his hand. That told me he had been associated with the sea. But he had a military bearing, however, and regulation side whiskers. Thus we have the Marine. He was a man with some amount of self-importance and a certain air of command. You must have observed the way he held his head and swung his cane. A steady, respectable, middle-aged man, too — all facts which led me to believe that he had been a sergeant."

"Extraordinary, Holmes!"

"Commonplace," replied Holmes, though I thought from his expression that he was pleased at my surprise and admiration.

"I said just now that there were no criminals. It appears that I'm wrong — look at this!"

He threw me over the note the commissionaire had brought. "Why," I cried, as I read it, "this is terrible!"

"It does seem to be a little out of the ordinary," he remarked, calmly. "Would you mind reading it to me aloud?"

This is the letter which I read to him:

" 'My dear Mr Sherlock Holmes,

There has been a bad business during the night at 3, Lauriston Gardens, off the Brixton Road. Our man on the beat saw a light there about two in the morning and as the house was empty, suspected that something was amiss. He found the door open, and in the front room, which is bare of furniture, discovered the body of a gentleman, well dressed, and having cards in his pocket bearing the name of 'Enoch J Drebber, Cleveland, Ohio, USA'.

" 'There had been no robbery, nor is there any evidence as to how the man met his death. There are marks of blood in the room, but there is no wound on the body. We are at a loss as to how he came into the empty house. Indeed the whole affair is a puzzler. If you can come round to the house any time before twelve, you will find me there. I have left everything as I found it. If you are unable to come, I shall give you fuller details, and would esteem it a great kindness if you would favour me with your opinion.

Yours faithfully,
TOBIAS GREGSON.' "

"Gregson is the smartest of the Scotland Yard detectives," Holmes remarked. "He and Lestrade are the best of a bad bunch. They are

quick and energetic, but conventional — shockingly so. They have their knives into each other, too. There will be some fun over this case if they are both working on it."

I was amazed at the calm way in which Holmes spoke. "Surely there is not a moment to be lost!" I said. "Shall I go and order you a cab?"

"I'm not sure whether I shall go. I'm the most incurably lazy devil sometimes."

"But it's just the chance you've been waiting for."

"My dear Watson, what does it matter to me? Suppose I do unravel the whole matter. You can be sure that Gregson and Lestrade will take all the credit. That comes of my being an unofficial investigator."

"But Gregson begs you to help him."

"Yes. He knows that I am his superior, but he would rather cut his tongue out than admit it to anyone. However, we may as well go and have a look. I shall work it out myself, I have no doubt. I may have a laugh at them, if I have nothing else. Come on, get your hat!"

"You wish me to come?"

"Yes, if you have nothing better to do."

A minute later we were both in a hansom cab heading furiously for the Brixton Road.

It was a dull, cloudy day and a veil seemed to hang over the roof-tops looking like the reflection of the mud-coloured streets below. Holmes seemed in the best of spirits and prattled on about the virtues of various makes of violin — a subject I knew of old that, next to the science of detection, was close to his heart.

"You don't seem to give much thought to the matter in hand," I said at last, interrupting him.

"No data yet," he answered. "It's a common mistake to theorize before you have all the evidence. It biases the judgment."

"You will have your data soon," I remarked, pointing with my finger; "this is the Brixton Road, and that's the house, if I am not very much mistaken."

"So it is. Stop, driver, stop!" We were still a hundred yards or so from the house, but Holmes insisted on our getting out and finishing the journey on foot.

"There goes another man in London who thinks you're mad," I said after paying the driver.

"Perhaps you should have told him you are my doctor, Watson."

Number 3, Lauriston Gardens, had an ill-omened look about it. A small garden, sprinkled with a few sickly plants, separated the house from the street and was crossed by a narrow path, yellowish in colour, and consisting of a mixture of clay and gravel. The whole place was very wet and sticky from the rain which had fallen through the night.

I had imagined that Sherlock Holmes would at once have hurried into the house and plunged himself into a study of the mystery. But nothing appeared to be further from his intention. Instead, he sauntered up and down the pavement outside the house, gazing vacantly at the ground, then the sky, then the houses opposite and finally at the railings in front of the house.

Having finished his scrutiny, Holmes proceeded slowly down the path, keeping his eyes riveted on the ground. Twice he stopped and once I saw him smile and heard him give a grunt of satisfaction. There were many marks of footsteps on the wet, clayey soil, but since the police had obviously been coming and going over it, I was unable to see how Holmes could hope to learn anything from it at all.

At the door of the house we were met by a white-faced man who rushed forward and wrung Holmes' hand with great energy. "It's very kind of you to come," he said. "I've left everything as it was. Nothing's been touched."

"Except that!" Holmes answered, pointing at the pathway. "If a herd of buffaloes had passed along there could not be a greater mess. No doubt you had drawn your conclusions, Gregson, before you permitted this."

"I — I've had so much to do — inside the house, I mean. My colleague, Mr Lestrade, is here. I had relied on him to look after the outside."

"With the two of you involved in the case, I wouldn't have thought there was much I could find out," said Holmes, raising his eyebrows.

"I think we've done all that can be done," answered Gregson, rubbing his hands together in a self-satisfied way. "It's a queer case, though, and I knew your taste for such things."

"You did not come here in a cab?" asked Holmes.

"No, sir."

"Nor Lestrade?"

"No, sir."

"Then let us go and look at the room." And with that, he strode into the house, followed by an astonished Inspector Gregson.

A short passage, bare-planked and dusty, led to the dining-room in which the mysterious affair had occurred. Holmes walked in and I followed. It was a large square room, looking all the larger from the absence of all furniture. It was a dingy, grimy, room with wallpaper, blotched with mildew, and torn in places, exposing the plaster beneath. Opposite the door was a fireplace, with a mantelpiece, on one corner of which was stuck the stump of a red wax candle.

All these details I observed later. At present my attention was centred on the single, grim, motionless figure stretched out on the floor-boards with vacant, sightless eyes staring up at the discoloured ceiling. A top hat was placed on the floor beside him. On his face there was an expression of horror, and, as it seemed to me, of hatred, such as I have never seen upon human features. I have seen death in many forms in my time, but never has it appeared to me in a more fearsome aspect than in that dark, depressing London house.

Lestrade, lean and ferret-like as ever, was standing by the doorway and greeted my companion and myself. "This case will make a stir. It beats anything that I've seen, and I'm no chicken."

"You've found no clue?" asked Gregson.

"None at all," replied Lestrade.

Sherlock Holmes approached the body, and, kneeling down, began to examine it closely. "You are sure that there is no wound?" he asked, pointing to the numerous splashes of blood which lay all around.

"Positive!" cried Gregson.

"Then, of course, this blood belongs to a second individual — presumably the murderer, if murder has been committed."

As he spoke, his nimble fingers moved rapidly over the body, feeling, pressing, unbut-toning, examining, while his eyes wore the same faraway look which I have already re-marked upon. Finally, he sniffed the dead man's lips, and then glanced at the soles of his patent-leather boots.

"He has not been moved at all?" he asked.

"No more than was necessary for the purpo-ses of our examination," answered Gregson.

"You can take him to the mortuary now," he said. "There's nothing more to be learned."

Gregson had a stretcher and two men at hand. At his call they entered the room, and the body was lifted and carried out. As it was raised, a ring tinkled down and rolled across the floor. Lestrade grabbed it and stared at it with mystified eyes.

"There's been a woman here," he cried. "It's a woman's wedding-ring." He held it out as he spoke, on the palm of his hand. We all gathered round him and gazed at it. There could be no doubt that it was a plain gold wedding-ring of the sort that had once adorned the finger of a bride.

"This complicates matters," said Gregson. "Heaven knows, they were complicated enough before."

"You're sure it doesn't simplify them?" observed Holmes. "Certainly there's nothing to be learned by staring at it. What did you find in the dead man's pockets?"

"We have it all here," said Gregson, pointing to a collection of objects on one of the bottom steps of the stairs. "A gold watch purchased from Barraud of London; gold watch-chain, very heavy and solid; gold ring; gold tie-pin; a leather pocket case with cards of 'Enoch J Drebber of Cleveland', corresponding with the 'E J D' on the handkerchief. No purse, but loose money to the extent of seven pounds and thirteen shillings. And two letters — one addressed to 'E J Drebber' and the other to 'Joseph Stangerson'."

"At what address?"

"American Exchange, Strand — to be left

until called for. Both letters are from the Atlantic Steamship Company, and refer to the sailing of their boats from Liverpool. It is clear that this unfortunate man was about to return to New York."

"Have you made any enquiries about this Stangerson?"

"I did so at once, of course. I've had an advertisement sent to all the newspapers, and one of my men has gone to the American Exchange, but he hasn't returned yet."

"Have you telegraphed Cleveland?"

"Yes, this morning."

"How did you word the telegram?"

"Simply asking for information that may assist us in our enquiries."

"You didn't ask for details on any point which appeared to you to be crucial?"

"I asked about Stangerson, naturally."

"Nothing else? Is there no circumstance on which this whole case appears to hinge? Will you not telegraph again?"

"I've said all I have to say," said Gregson, in an offended voice.

Sherlock Holmes chuckled to himself, and was about to say something, when Lestrade, who had returned to the dining-room while we stood talking in the hall, reappeared, rubbing

his hands and looking well satisfied.

"Mr Gregson," he said, "I've just made a discovery of the highest importance, and one which would have been overlooked had I not made a very careful examination of the walls." Lestrade's eyes sparkled as he spoke, and he was obviously pleased at having scored a point against his colleague.

"Come here," he said, bustling back into the dining-room. "Now, stand there!" We did as he said. And pointing proudly at the wall Lestrade said, "Look at that!"

I have remarked that the paper had fallen away in parts. In this particular corner of the room a large piece had peeled off and below it was scrawled a single word: *Rache.*

"What do you think of that?" cried Lestrade. "This was overlooked because it was in the darkest corner of the room, and no one thought of looking there."

"And what does it mean now that you have found it?" asked Gregson.

"Mean? Why, man, it means that the writer was going to write the female name *Rachel*, but was disturbed before he or she had time to finish. You mark my words, when this case comes to be cleared up you will find that a

woman named Rachel has something to do with it.

"It's all very well for you to laugh, Mr Sherlock Holmes. You may be very smart and clever, but the old hound is the best, when all's said and done."

"I really do beg your pardon!" said Holmes, who had indeed exploded into loud laughter. "You certainly have the credit of being the first of us to find this out and, as you say, it bears every mark of having been written by the other participant in last night's mystery. I have not

had time to examine this room yet, but with your permission I shall do so now."

As he spoke, he whipped a tape measure and a large magnifying glass from his coat pocket. With these he walked silently about the room, sometimes stopping, occasionally kneeling, and once lying flat on his face. So engrossed was he that he appeared to have forgotten our presence, for he chattered away to himself under his breath the whole time.

For twenty minutes or more he continued his researches, measuring with the most exact care the distance between marks which were entirely invisible to me, and occasionally applying his tape to the walls in an equally incomprehensible manner. In one place he gathered up very carefully a little pile of grey dust from the floor, and packed it away in an envelope. Finally he examined with his glass the word upon the wall, going over every letter with the most minute exactness. This done, he appeared to be satisfied, for he replaced his tape and magnifying glass in his pocket.

"They say that genius is an infinite capacity for taking pains," he remarked with a smile. "It's a very bad definition, but it certainly applies to detective work."

Gregson and Lestrade had watched the antics of their amateur colleague with considerable curiosity and some contempt. "Well what do you think of it, sir?" they asked.

"It would be robbing you of the credit of the case if I was to presume to help you," replied Holmes, sarcastically. "But if you let me know how your investigations go, I'll be happy to assist you in any way I can. In the meantime I should like to speak to the constable who found the body. Can you give me his name and address."

Lestrade glanced at his notebook. "Let me see. Ah, yes. John Rance. But you won't need his address; he's on duty outside."

"Come along, Doctor, we must interview

Rance without delay."

Before leaving, however, Holmes turned to the two detectives and said, "There has been murder done, and the murderer was a man. He was more than six feet tall, and was in the prime of life, had small feet for his height, and wore square-toed boots. He came here with the victim in a four-wheeled cab, which was drawn by a horse with three old shoes and one new one. The murderer in all probability has remarkably long fingernails on his right hand. These are only a few indications, but they may assist you. Good day, gentlemen."

Lestrade and Gregson glanced at each other and smiled.

"If this man was murdered," asked Lestrade, "how was it done?"

"Poison," replied Holmes, curtly, and strode off. "One other thing, Lestrade," he added, turning round at the door. "*Rache* is the German for 'revenge'; so don't waste your time looking for Miss Rachel."

And with this he walked away, leaving the two rivals open-mouthed behind him.

2 What John Rance Had to Tell

Striding out of the house, Sherlock Holmes went straight up to the policeman stationed by the front gate. "Constable Rance, you discovered the body, I understand?"

"Yes, sir. First upon the scene, sir. I've made my report."

"We thought we should like to hear it all from your own lips," said Holmes, "if you don't mind."

"Very well, sir, I'll tell it from the beginning. My duty shift is generally from ten at night to six in the morning. Around two o'clock or a little after I thought I'd take a look down the Brixton Road to see that all was right. It was a filthy night — raining cats and dogs — and lonely on the beat. Not a soul did I meet all the way down, though a cab or two went past. Well, strolling down the road I suddenly saw a glint of a light in the window of a house in Lauriston Gardens that I knew was empty. I was real surprised at seeing a light in the window, and suspected as something was wrong. When I got to the door . . ."

"You stopped, and then walked back to the garden gate," interrupted Holmes. "What did you do that for?"

Rance gave a start and stared at Holmes with the utmost amazement. "Why, that's right enough, sir, though how you come to know it, heaven only knows. You see, when I got to the front door it was so still and quiet like that I thought I'd be none the worse for having someone with me. So I walked back to the gate to see if I could see PC Murcher's lantern. But there wasn't no sign of him nor anyone else."

"There was no one in the street?"

"Not a living soul, sir, nor as much as a dog. Then I pulled myself together and went back and pushed the door open. All was quiet inside, so I went into the room where the light was a-burning. There was a candle flickering on the mantelpiece — a red wax one — and by its light I saw —".

"Yes, I know what you saw. You walked round the room several times, and you knelt down by the body, and then you walked through and tried the kitchen door, and then —".

"Where was you hid to see all that?" Rance cried. "It seems to me you know a lot more than you should."

"I'm not the murderer, if that's what you're thinking," laughed Holmes. "Go on please, Rance. What did you do next?"

Rance resumed, without, however, losing his startled expression. "I went back to the gate and blew my whistle. That brought Murcher to the spot."

"Was the street empty then?"

"Well, it was, as far as anybody that could be of any good goes."

"What do you mean?"

The policeman's features broadened into a grin. "I've seen many a drunk in my time," he said, " but never anyone as drunk as that cove. He was at the gate when I came out, leaning up against the railings, a-singin' and a-swayin' in all directions. He couldn't even stand, far less walk straight."

"What sort of man was he?" asked Sherlock Holmes, with sudden interest.

PC Rance appeared to be somewhat irritated by this question. "He was an uncommon drunk sort o'man," he said.

"His face — his clothes — didn't you notice them?"

"I should think I did notice them, seeing that I had to prop him up. He was a tall chap, the lower part of his face was muffled — "

"That will do," cried Holmes. "What became of him?"

"We'd enough to do without looking after him," the policeman said, in an aggrieved voice. "I'll wager he found his way home all right."

"How was he dressed?"

"A brown overcoat."

"You didn't happen to see or hear a cab after that?"

"No."

"I'm afraid, Rance, that you will never rise in the force. That head of yours should be for use as well as ornament. You might have gained your sergeant's stripes last night. The man you held in your hands is the man who holds the clue to this mystery, and the man we are seeking. There's no use arguing about it now; I tell you that it is so. Come along, Doctor, we can do nothing more here."

It was one o'clock when we left 3 Lauriston Gardens. Sherlock Holmes led me to the nearest telegraph office, where he despatched a long telegram. He then hailed a cab, and ordered the driver to take us home.

"That blundering fool Rance!" he said, as we seated ourselves in the cab. "Just to think of his having such an incomparable bit of luck, and not taking advantage of it. Still, my mind is entirely made up about this case."

"Really, Holmes, you amaze me. Surely you're not as sure as you pretended to be of all those particulars you gave Lestrade and Gregson?"

"Pretence, Watson? There was no pretence. There's absolutely no room for mistake. The very first thing I observed on arriving was that a cab had made two ruts with its wheels close to the kerb. Now, up to last night, we have had no rain for a week, so those wheels which left such a deep impression must have been there during the night. There were the marks of the horses hoofs, too, the outline of one far more clearly cut than that of the other three, showing that it

was a new shoe. Since the cab was there after the rain began, and was not there at any time during the morning — I have Gregson's word for that — it follows that it must have been there during the night, and, therefore, that it must have brought those two individuals to the house."

"That seems simple enough," I said, "but how about the other man's height?"

"Why, the height of a man, in nine cases out of ten, can be told from the length of his stride. It's a simple calculation enough, though there's no point in boring you with the figures. I was able to measure this fellow's stride both on the clay outside and on the dust within. Then I had a way of checking my calculation. When a man writes on a wall, his instinct leads him to write about the level of his own eyes. Now that writing was just over six feet from the ground. It was child's play."

"And his age?"

"Well, if a man can stride four and a half feet without the slightest effort, he must be pretty fit. That was the breadth of a puddle on the

garden path which he had evidently walked across. Patent-leather boots had gone round, and square-toed boots had hopped over. Is there anything else that puzzles you?"

"The finger nails," I suggested.

"The writing on the wall was done with a man's forefinger. My glass allowed me to observe that the wallpaper was slightly scratched in doing it, which would not have been the case if the man's nails had been trimmed. It is in such details that the skilled detective differs from the Gregsons and Lestrades of this world."

"My head is in a whirl; the more one thinks of it the more mysterious it grows. How came those two men — if there were two men — into an empty house? What has become of the cabman who drove them? How could one man compel another to take poison? Where did the blood come from? What was the motive of the murderer, since robbery had no part in it? How came the woman's ring there? Above all, why should the second man write up the German word *Rache* before leaving? I confess that I cannot see any possible way of reconciling all these facts."

Holmes smiled approvingly. "You sum up the difficulties of the case admirably, my dear Watson. There is much that is still obscure, though I have quite made up my mind on the main facts."

"I'm still in the dark, I must confess. True, your description of the second man seems to tally with what Rance said, but why should he come back to the house after leaving it? That is not the way of criminals, surely?"

"The ring, man, the ring! That was what he came back for. If we have no other way of catching him, we can always bait our man with the ring. I shall have him, Watson — I'll bet you two to one that I have him. And I must thank you for it. I might not have gone but for you. There's the scarlet thread of murder running through this episode: a study in scarlet, one might say. And our duty is to unravel it, and expose every inch of it. And now for lunch."

The cab by now had arrived back at our lodgings in Baker Street. As we went in, I could not help but express my profound admiration for the skill that my companion had already shown in handling the case.

"You have brought detection as near an exact science as it ever will be brought in this world," I said. And the obvious pleasure that my words gave him showed that he was not as insensitive to flattery as he would wish to make out.

3   We Have a Visitor

After lunch that day, Holmes announced that he had to go out and that he would not return until the evening, for there was a concert that he very much wanted to attend.

It was indeed late before he returned that evening, so late — about seven o'clock — that I knew the concert could not have detained him all the time.

"It was magnificent!" he said on taking his usual chair. "But, my dear chap, what on earth is the matter? You're not looking quite yourself. Has this Brixton Road affair upset you?"

"To tell the truth, Holmes, it has. I ought to be more hardened I know, particularly after my experiences in Afghanistan when I saw my comrades hacked to pieces without losing my nerve. But this affair —".

"I can understand perfectly. There is a mystery about this which stimulates the imagination; and without imagination there is no horror. Have you seen the evening paper?"

"Why, no."

"It gives a fairly good account of the Lauriston Gardens affair. It does not mention the fact that when the man was raised up a woman's wedding-ring fell onto the floor. It is just as well it does not."

"Why?"

"Look at this advertisement," he answered. "I had one sent to every newspaper immediately after lunch."

Holmes threw the paper across to me and I glanced at the place marked:

FOUND IN BRIXTON ROAD THIS MORNING A PLAIN GOLD WEDDING RING APPLY: DR. WATSON 221B BAKER ST. BETWEEN 8:00 AND 9:00 THIS EVENING

"Excuse my using your name," he said.

"That's all right. But supposing anyone applies — I have no ring."

"Oh, yes, you have," said he, handing me one. "This will do very well. It's almost identical."

"And who do you expect will answer this advertisement?"

"Why the man in the brown coat — our friend with the square-toes. If he doesn't come himself, he'll send an accomplice."

"Would he not consider it too dangerous?"

"Not at all. If my view of the case is correct, and I have every reason to believe that it is, this man would rather risk anything than lose the ring. I believe that he dropped it while stooping over Drebber's body, and did not miss it at the time. After leaving the house he discovered his loss and hurried back, but found the police already there, owing to his having left the candle burning. He had to pretend to be drunk in order to allay the suspicions which might have been aroused by his appearance at the front gate.

"Now put yourself in that man's place. On thinking the matter over, it must have occurred to him that he had lost the ring in the road after leaving the house. What would he do then? He would eagerly look out for the papers in the hope of seeing it among the articles found. His eye, of course, would alight upon this. He

would be overjoyed. Why should he fear a trap? There would be no reason in his eyes why the finding of the ring should be connected with the murder. He would come. He *will* come."

"And then?"

"Oh, you can leave me to deal with him. Have your revolver ready, cleaned and loaded. He will be a desperate man, and though I shall take him unawares, it is as well to be ready for anything."

I went to my room and followed Holmes' advice. When I returned with the pistol, the table had been cleared and Holmes was playing his violin.

"I have just had an answer to my telegram," he said as I entered. "As I suspected, my view of the case is the correct one."

"And that is?" I asked eagerly.

"My fiddle would be the better for new strings," he remarked. It was obvious that he was unwilling to share his view of the case with me, correct or otherwise. But just at that moment, there was a sharp ring at the front door.

"Now, Watson. Put your pistol in your pocket, and speak to him in an ordinary way. Leave the rest to me. Don't frighten him by looking at him too hard."

I quickly descended the stairs to the front door. Opening it, instead of the man of violence whom we had both expected, a very old and wrinkled woman stood gazing up at me. She appeared to be dazzled by the sudden blaze of

light, and after giving a curtsy, she stood blinking and fumbling in her pocket with nervous shaky fingers.

The old woman drew out a newspaper and pointed at our advertisement. "It's this as has brought me, sir; a gold wedding-ring lost in the Brixton Road. It belongs to my girl Sally, as was married only this time a year ago. Her husband's a steward aboard a Union Steamship and what he'd say if he come 'ome and found her without her ring is more than I dare think about, he being short tempered at the best o' times —"

"Is that her ring?" I asked.

"The Lord be thanked!" cried the old woman. "Sally will be a glad woman this night. Yes, sir, that's the ring."

"And what may your address be?"

"13, Duncan Street, Houndsditch. A long and weary way from here, sir."

"And your name?"

"My name's Sawyer, sir — hers is Mrs Dennis."

"Here is your ring, Mrs Sawyer. It clearly belongs to your daughter, and I am glad to be able to restore it to the rightful owner."

With many mumbled blessings and thanks, the old woman packed the ring into her pocket and shuffled off down the street. The moment I closed the front door, Sherlock Holmes quickly put on his coat and hat and said, "I'll follow her. She must be an accomplice and will lead me to him. Wait up for me."

Looking through the window from upstairs, I could see the old woman walking feebly along the other side of the street with Holmes some little distance behind her. "Either his whole theory is incorrect," I thought to myself, "or else he will be led now to the heart of the mystery."

Certainly there was no need for Holmes to ask me to wait up for him, for I felt that sleep was impossible until I heard the result of his adventure. It was close upon nine when Holmes had set out. I had no idea how long he might be, so I sat puffing at my pipe and skipping

over the pages of a book. Ten o'clock passed; eleven o'clock struck. It was close on twelve before I heard the sharp sound of a key being turned in the front door. The instant Holmes entered I could see by his face that he had not been successful. But when he slumped into his armchair he burst into a hearty laugh.

"I wouldn't have Gregson and Lestrade know it for the world," he cried. "I have laughed at them so much that they would never let me hear the end of it. I can laugh now because I know that I will get even with them in the long run."

"What's happened then?"

"Oh, I don't mind telling you, Watson. That old woman had gone only a little way when she began to limp and show signs of being footsore. Presently she came to a halt and hailed a cab which was passing. I managed to be close to her so as to hear the address, but I need not have been so anxious, for she sang it out loud enough to be heard at the other side of the street: 'Drive to 13, Duncan Street, Houndsditch,' she cried.

"Having seen her safely inside the cab, I perched myself behind. Well, away we rattled and didn't stop until we reached the street in question. I hopped off before we came to the door, and strolled down the street. I saw the cab pull up. The driver jumped down, and I saw him open the door and stand expectantly. Nothing came out though. When I reached him, he was groping away frantically in the empty cab. There was no sign or trace of his passenger, and I fear it will be some time before he gets his fare. On inquiring at Number 13 we found that the house belonged to a decorator, named Keswick, and that no one of the name either of Sawyer or Dennis had ever been heard of there."

"You mean to say that that tottering, feeble old woman was able to get out of the cab while it was in motion, without either you or the driver seeing her?"

"Old woman be damned!" said Holmes sharply. "We were the old women to be so taken in. It must have been a man in the prime of life, and an active one too, beside being an incomparable actor. The disguise certainly fooled us. He saw that he was followed, no doubt, and used this means of giving me the slip. It shows that the man we are after is not as lonely as I imagined he was, but has friends who are ready to risk something for him. Now, Doctor, you look all done-in. Take my advice and go to bed."

I was certainly feeling weary, so I did as Holmes suggested. I left him in front of the smouldering fire, and long into the night I heard the low, sad sound of his violin, and knew that he was still pondering over the strange problem which he had set himself to unravel.

4   Inspector Gregson Shows What He Can Do

The papers next day were full of the 'Brixton Mystery', as they termed it. Interestingly, there was some information in them that was new to me. The *Standard* stated that the deceased had stayed at the boarding-house of Madame Charpentier, in Torquay Terrace, Camberwell, with his secretary, Mr Joseph Stangerson. The two had left their lodgings on Tuesday for Euston Station with the intention of catching the train to Liverpool. They were later seen on the platform, but nothing more was heard of them until Mr Drebber's body was discovered in an empty house in the Brixton Road, many miles from Euston. How he came there, or how he met his fate, is still shrouded in mystery. Nothing is known of the whereabouts of Stangerson.

A number of the papers also commented that they were glad to learn that Mr Lestrade and Mr Gregson, of Scotland Yard, were both engaged on the case and confidently predicted that it was just a matter of time before these two well-known officers solved the mystery.

Sherlock Holmes and I read these pieces over breakfast and they seemed to provide him with considerable amusement.

"I told you that whatever happened, Lestrade and Gregson would be bound to score."

"That depends on how it turns out, surely."

"It doesn't matter in the least. If the man is caught, it will be *on account* of their efforts; if he escapes, it will be *in spite* of their exertions. Its heads I win and tails you lose."

"What on earth is that?" I cried suddenly, for at this moment there came a pattering of many steps in the hall and on the stairs, accompanied by audible expressions of disgust on the part of

our housekeeper, Mrs Hudson.

"What on earth is that?" I cried, for at that moment the door was flung open and in rushed four of the dirtiest and most ragged street urchins that I had ever seen.

"It's the Baker Street division of the detective police force," answered Holmes gravely. " 'Tention!"

Instantly the four dirty scoundrels stood in a line. "In future you shall send Wiggins alone to report, and the rest of you must wait in the street. Have you found it, Wiggins?"

"No, sir, we ain't," said one of the boys.

"I hardly expected you would. You must keep on until you do. Here are your wages." He handed each one of them a shilling. "Now, off you go, and come back with a better report next time."

He waved his hand, and they scampered away downstairs like so many rats, and we heard their shrill voices next moment in the street below.

"There's more work to be got out of those little beggars than out of a dozen of the regular police force," Holmes remarked. "The mere sight of an official-looking person seals men's lips. These youngsters, however, go everywhere, and hear everything. They are as sharp as needles, too."

"Is it on this Brixton case that you are employing them?"

"Yes; there is a point which I wish to ascertain. Hullo! I think we are about to hear something now. Here's Gregson coming down the road with self-satisfaction written on every feature of his face. Bound for us, I suppose. Yes, he's stopping. Here he is."

There was a violent ringing at the front-door bell and in a few moments Mrs Hudson had shown Inspector Gregson upstairs.

"My dear fellow," he said, wringing Holmes's unresponsive hand. "Congratulate me! I have made the whole thing as clear as day."

"You mean to say that you are now on the right track?" asked Holmes, a shade of anxiety appearing on his face.

"The right track! Why, sir, we have the man under lock and key."

"May I ask his name?"

"Arthur Charpentier, sub-lieutenant in Her Majesty's Royal Navy."

Sherlock Holmes gave a sigh of relief and relaxed into a smile.

"Take a seat and try one of these cigars," he said. "We're anxious to know how you managed it. Will you have some whisky."

"No thank you, Mr Holmes, not while I'm on duty."

Gregson was clearly feeling very pleased with himself and could not stop chuckling and saying, "The fun of it is, that that fool Lestrade, who thinks himself so smart, has gone off on the wrong track altogether! He's after Stangerson, Drebber's secretary, who had no more to do with the crime than an unborn babe. I've no doubt he's caught him by now." And the idea tickled Gregson so much that he laughed until he almost choked.

"I'll tell you all about it, strictly between ourselves, of course. The first difficulty was finding out about this Drebber's background. Some people would have waited until their advertisements were answered," and here he gave Holmes a shifty look, "but this is not Tobias Gregson's way of doing things. Now, you remember that hat beside the dead man?"

"Yes," said Holmes, "it was made by John Underwood and Sons, 129, Camberwell Road."

"I had no idea that you noticed that," said Gregson. "Have you been there?"

"No."

"Ha!" cried Gregson, obviously relieved. "You should never neglect a chance you know, however small it may seem."

"To a great mind, nothing is little," remarked Holmes.

"Well, I went to Underwood and asked him to whom he had sold the hat, giving him the size and description. Looking it up in his books he discovered that it had been sold, as I knew,

of course, to a Mr Drebber who was staying at Charpentier's Boarding House, Torquay Terrace, Camberwell. Thus I got his address."

"Smart — very smart!" murmured Holmes.

"I then called at Torquay Terrace and found Madame Charpentier very pale and distressed. Her daughter was in the room — an uncommonly fine girl she is too. 'You have heard of the mysterious death of your late boarder Mr Enoch J Drebber of Cleveland?' I asked her. She nodded. The daughter burst into tears. These people obviously knew something about the matter and I began to smell a rat.

"Well, I asked the mother what time Drebber had left on the night of his murder. 'Eight o'clock she said. His secretary, Mr Stangerson, said that there were two trains — one at 9.15 and one at 11. He was to catch the first.'

" 'And that was the last you saw of him?' I asked. A terrible change came over her when I asked the question. It was some seconds before she could get out the single word 'Yes' — and when it did come it was in a husky, unnatural tone. There was a moment's silence, and then the daughter spoke in a calm, clear voice.

" 'No good can ever come of telling lies, mother,' she said. 'We did see Mr Drebber again.'

" 'God forgive you!' cried Madame Charpentier, throwing up her hands in horror. 'You have murdered your brother.'

" 'You'd better tell me all about it now,' I said.

" 'On your head be it, Alice!' cried the mother. Then turning to me she said, 'I'll tell you all, sir. Perhaps, Alice, you had better leave us together.' At this the daughter withdrew. 'Mr Drebber was with us nearly three weeks,' she began. 'He and his secretary, Mr Stangerson, had been travelling on the continent. Stangerson was a quiet, reserved man, but his employer, I'm sorry to say, was quite different. The very night of his arrival he became very much the worse for drink. He was coarse in his manners and brutish in his ways. Worse, he became very familiar towards my daughter, Alice. On one occasion he actually seized her in his arms and embraced her.'

" 'But why did you stand for it?' I asked. 'I suppose you can get rid of your lodgers when you wish?'

" 'I'm a poor widow, sir, and my boy in the

Navy has cost me much. I needed the money. I acted for the best. But this last was too much and I gave him notice to leave. That was the reason for his going.'

" 'What happened then?'

" 'Though I was relieved at his going, it was less than an hour later that he returned. He was very excited and obviously drunk. He pushed me aside and forced his way into the room where my daughter was sitting. There, before my very eyes, he proposed that she run away with him. "I have money enough to spare," he said. "Never mind about the old girl here, come with me and you shall live like a princess." Poor Alice was so frightened that she shrunk away from him, but Drebber caught her by the wrist and dragged her towards the door. I screamed and at that moment my son Arthur came into the room.

" 'What happened then, I don't know. I heard shouting and the confused sounds of a scuffle. I was too terrified to raise my head, but when I did I saw Arthur standing in the doorway

laughing, with a stick in his hand. "I don't think he'll be troubling us again," he said. "I'll just go after him and see what he does," and with these words he started off down the street. The next morning we heard of Mr Drebber's mysterious death.'

"This statement," continued Gregson, "I took down myself in shorthand so there should be no mistakes."

"How exciting," said Holmes with a yawn. "What happened next?"

"I saw that the whole case rested on one point. So, fixing her with my eye, I asked her at what hour her son returned.

" 'I don't know,' she answered.

" 'Not know?'

" 'No; he has his own key and he let himself in.'

" 'After you went to bed?'

" 'Yes.'

" 'When did you get to bed?'

" 'About eleven.'

" 'So your son was gone at least two hours?'

" 'Yes.'

" 'Possibly four or five?'

" 'Yes.'

" 'What was he doing during that time?'

" 'I don't know,' she answered, turning white.

"Of course after that there was nothing more to be done. I found out where Lieutenant Charpentier was, took two officers with me, and arrested him. When I touched him on the shoulder and told him to come quietly, he said, 'I suppose you are arresting me for being concerned with the death of that scoundrel Drebber?' Very suspicious, I thought, since we hadn't mentioned it."

"Very," said Holmes.

"And he still carried the heavy stick which his mother described him as having with him when he followed Drebber."

"What is your theory, then?" asked Holmes, in a bored voice.

"Well, my theory is that he followed Drebber as far as the Brixton Road. There a fresh argument arose between them, in the course of which Drebber received a blow from the stick, in the pit of the stomach perhaps, which killed him without leaving any mark. Charpentier then dragged Drebber's body into the empty house. As to the candle, and the blood, and the writing on the wall, and the ring, they may all have been planted to throw the police on to the wrong scent."

"Well!" said Holmes in an encouraging voice. "Really, Gregson, you are getting along! We shall make something of you yet."

"I flatter myself that I managed it rather well," Gregson answered proudly. "Charpentier, of course, denies everything. He says after following Drebber he saw him get into a cab. Deciding to return home, Charpentier then happened to meet an old shipmate of his, and together they took a long walk. When I asked him where this old shipmate lived, he was

unable to give me a satisfactory reply. I think the whole case fits together very well. And to think that Lestrade is on the completely wrong track! Why, talk of the devil, here's Lestrade now!"

It was indeed Lestrade, who having been shown up by Mrs Hudson, now entered. His face was disturbed and troubled. He stood in the centre of the room, fumbling nervously with his hat. "This is the most extraordinary case," he said at last — "a most incomprehensible affair."

"Ah, you think so, Lestrade?" cried Gregson, triumphantly. "I thought you would come to that conclusion. Have you managed to find the secretary, Mr Stangerson?"

"Mr Joseph Stangerson," said Lestrade, gravely, "was murdered at Halliday's Private Hotel about six o'clock this morning."

5 Light in the Darkness

The news with which Lestrade greeted us was so momentous and unexpected that we were all three fairly dumbfounded. Gregson sprang out of his chair, I stared in silence and Holmes, frowning, muttered, "Stangerson too! The plot thickens."

"Are you — are you sure of this?" stammered Gregson.

"I've just come from his room," said Lestrade. "I was the first to discover what happened."

"We've just been hearing Gregson's view of the case," said Holmes. "Would you mind telling us what you have seen and done?"

"I've no objection, no," answered Lestrade, sitting down. "I confess that I thought Stangerson was involved in the death of Drebber. This fresh development has shown me that I was completely mistaken. I knew that Stangerson had been seen with Drebber at Euston Station at about eight-thirty on the night of Drebber's death. What happened to Stangerson after that time? That was the question I was determined to find an answer to.

"I telegraphed to Liverpool, giving a description of the man, and warning them to keep a watch on the boats leaving for America. I then set to work calling on all hotels and lodging-houses close to Euston Station, thinking that if Drebber and Stangerson had become separated, the natural thing for Stangerson would have been to stay somewhere in the vicinity for the night and to have met Drebber again the next day."

"They would probably have agreed on some meeting place beforehand," remarked Holmes.

"And so it proved. I spent the whole of yesterday making inquiries, but with no success at all. This morning I began very early, and at eight o'clock reached Halliday's Private Hotel, in Little George Street. I discovered that Stangerson was staying there.

" 'No doubt you are the gentleman Mr Stangerson has been expecting for two days,' the man at the reception desk said.

" 'Where is he now?' I asked.

" 'He's upstairs in bed. He wished to be called at nine.'

" 'I'll go up and see him at once.' "

"I was shown up to the room, which was on the second floor. There I saw something that made me feel sick, in spite of my twenty years as a police officer. From under the door there curled a little red ribbon of blood. I gave a cry, which brought the boy who had shown me up, back smartly. He nearly fainted when he saw the blood.

"The door was locked from the inside, so together we put our shoulders to it and knocked it in. The window of the room was open and beside the window, all huddled up, lay the body of a man in his pyjamas. He was quite dead and had been so for some time, for he was rigid and cold. When we turned him over, the boy recognized him at once as Mr Stangerson.

"The cause of death was a deep stab wound in the left side, which must have penetrated the heart. And now comes the strangest thing. What do you think was above the murdered man?"

I felt a creeping of the flesh and a chill of horror, even before Sherlock Holmes answered, without hesitation, "The word *Rache*, scratched on the wall."

"That's it," said Lestrade, amazed. It was

several seconds before any one spoke, and then Lestrade continued. "I naturally began my inquiries, and soon discovered from the milkman that he had seen a ladder propped up against an open window on the second floor, at the back of the hotel. A little later he looked back and saw a man descend the ladder. He took no particular notice of him — thinking he was a carpenter or joiner at work — beyond thinking that it was early for the man to be at work. But he did form the impression that the man was tall and was dressed in a long, brownish coat. Whoever he was, he must have stayed in the room some time after the murder, for we found blood-stains in the wash-basin, where he had washed his hands, and marks on the sheets where he had deliberately wiped his knife."

On hearing the description of the murderer I glanced at Holmes. There was, however, no look of satisfaction on his face.

"Did you find anything in the room which could give a clue to the murderer?" he asked.

"Nothing. Stangerson had Drebber's purse in his pocket, but that doesn't strike me as strange, since he did all the paying. There was over eighty pounds in it. Whatever the motives of these crimes, robbery is clearly not one of them. There were no papers in the dead man's pockets or possessions except a telegram, dated from Cleveland about a month ago and containing the words, 'J H is in Europe'. There was no name on the telegram."

"And there was nothing else?" asked Holmes.

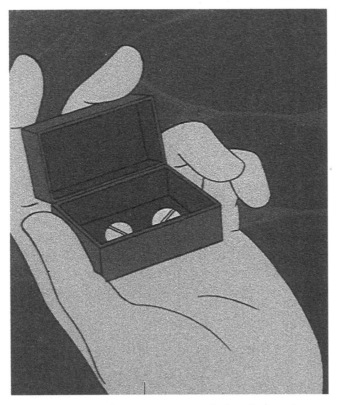

"Nothing of importance. A book, a pipe, a glass of water on the table and on the window-sill a small box containing a couple of pills."

Sherlock Holmes sprang from his chair with a cry of delight. "The last link! My case is complete."

Gregson and Lestrade looked at him in amazement.

"I have in my hands," said Holmes, confidently, "all the threads which have formed such a tangle. There are, of course, details to be filled in, but I'm as certain of all the main facts, from the time Drebber parted from Stangerson at the station up to the discovery of Drebber's body, as if I had seen them with my own eyes. I will give you proof of my knowledge. Could you lay your hands on those pills?"

"I have them with me," said Lestrade, producing a small box. "It was the merest chance my taking it for I don't attach any importance to them."

"Give them here," said Holmes. "Now, Doctor," he said turning to me, "are these ordinary pills?"

They certainly were not. They were of a pearly-grey colour, small, round and almost transparent against the light. "From their lightness and transparency," I said, "I should say they are soluble in water."

"Precisely so," answered Holmes. "Now

would you mind going down and fetching that poor old terrier that's been so ill so long and which Mrs Hudson wanted you to put out of its pain yesterday."

I went downstairs and carried the dog up in my arms. Its heavy breathing and glazed expression showed that it was not far from its end. I placed it upon a cushion on the rug.

"I'll now cut one of these pills in two," said Holmes, drawing out his penknife. "One half we return to the box for future purposes, the other half I'll place in this wine-glass with a teaspoonful of water. As you see, the Doctor is right and that it quickly dissolves."

"This is all very interesting," said Lestrade, "but I cannot see what it has to do with the death of Mr Joseph Stangerson."

"Patience, my friend, patience! You will find in time that it has everything to do with it. I shall now add a little milk to make the mixture palatable and on giving it to the dog he will lap it up readily enough."

As he spoke he turned the contents of the wine-glass into a saucer and placed it in front of the dog, who speedily licked it dry. We all sat in silence, watching the animal intently, expecting some startling effect. None appeared, however. The dog continued to lie stretched out on the cushion, still breathing with difficulty, but apparently neither the better nor worse for its medicine.

Holmes sat looking intently at his watch. As minute followed minute with no change in the dog he appeared bitterly disappointed. "It can't be a coincidence," he cried, springing from his chair and pacing up and down the room, "it's impossible. The very pills which I suspected in the Drebber case are actually found after the death of Stangerson. And yet they seem harmless. What can it mean? Surely my whole train of reasoning cannot have been wrong. It's impossible. And yet this dog is none the worse."

Continuing to pace the room in an agitated manner, while the two detectives smiled on derisively, Holmes eventually stopped and with a shriek of delight, rushed to the tiny pill box, shouting, "I have it! I have it!"

Cutting the other pill in two, he dissolved it in water, added milk and presented it to the terrier as before. The unfortunate creature's tongue seemed hardly to have moistened in it before it gave a convulsive shiver in every limb, and lay as rigid and lifeless as if it had been struck by lightning.

Drawing a deep breath, Holmes wiped the perspiration from his forehead. "I should have more faith," he said; "I ought to know by this time that when a fact appears to be opposed to a long train of deductions, it invariably proves capable of bearing some other interpretation. Of the two pills in the box, one was of the most deadly poison, and the other was entirely harmless. I ought to have known that before I had even seen the box."

What Holmes could have possibly meant by this was beyond my understanding. There was the dead dog, however, to prove that his conjecture — whatever it was — had been correct.

"All this seems strange to you all," he said, "because you failed at the beginning of the inquiry to grasp the importance of the single real clue which was presented to you. I had the good fortune to seize upon that, and everything which has occurred since then has served to confirm my original theory. Hence things which have baffled you and made the case more obscure have helped to clarify things for me and strengthen my conclusions."

"Look here," said Gregson, who had listened to Holmes with considerable impatience, "we all know you are smart and that you have your own methods of working. But we want something more than mere theory and preaching from you, you know. I admit that I was wrong about Charpentier, who obviously couldn't have been involved in this second murder. Lestrade went after this second man, Stangerson, and it seems that he was wrong too. You, meanwhile, have thrown out hints here, and hints there, and seem to know more than we do, but the time has come when we feel that we have the right to ask you straight how much you do know. Can you name the man who did it?"

"I can't help feeling that Gregson's right," remarked Lestrade. "We've both tried and both failed. You said more than once that

you've got all the evidence you require. So, who is he, then?"

"Any delay, Holmes," I added, "might give the murderer time to commit some fresh atrocity."

"There will be no more murders," said

Holmes, "you need have no fear of that. You have asked me if I know the murderer's name. I do. Just knowing his name, however, is a small thing compared to getting our hands on him. This I expect to do very shortly."

Gregson and Lestrade were both about to say something about this new and startling piece of information, when there was a tap on the door and young Wiggins, leader of the street gang, barged in.

"Please, sir," he said, "I've got the cab downstairs."

"Good boy, Wiggins," said Holmes, smiling. "Ask the cabman to step up, and give a hand with my luggage, will you?"

I was certainly surprised by what Holmes said, since this was the first that I had heard about his setting out on a journey. There was a small trunk in the room, however, and this he began to secure with a strap, as the cabman entered the room. "Give me a hand with this trunk, cabman," he said, kneeling down and fastening the buckle of the strap.

The cabman stepped forward and put a hand out to assist. In an instant there was a sharp click and the jangling of metal, as Sherlock Holmes clapped a pair of handcuffs on him. Then springing to his feet, Holmes cried, "Gentlemen, let me introduce you to Mr Jefferson Hope, the murderer of Enoch Drebber and of Joseph Stangerson!"

Everything occurred so quickly that it was several seconds before I realized what had happened. Gregson and Lestrade stood there too, like two stuffed dummies. But we were roused from our shock by the most terrible roar of fury. Wrenching himself free of Holmes' grasp, the prisoner made a desperate dash for the window. Before Holmes, Lestrade, Gregson or myself were able to stop him, Jefferson Hope hurled himself through the glass.

6 Jefferson Hope's Confession

Astonished, we rushed to the window and saw, in the street below, the prisoner lying in the gutter, writhing in pain. As quick as a flash, Holmes ran down to the road followed by myself, Lestrade and Gregson.

Incredibly, the prisoner was smiling. "I don't know who you are," he said as Holmes knelt down beside him, "but if there's a vacancy for chief of police, I reckon you're the man for the job. The way you tracked me down was a caution."

"Don't speak now," replied Holmes, "there's time enough for that. Gregson, get one of your men to fetch an ambulance. This man needs urgent attention, hurry."

The two detectives exchanged glances, but Gregson did as Holmes had asked. When the ambulance arrived, the prisoner was taken away with Gregson and Lestrade. Holmes hailed a cab saying, "Come on, Doctor, you've taken an interest in this case. You may as well hear it out to the end."

The prisoner was taken direct to hospital. While he was being attended to, Holmes and I waited outside his room until called in by Lestrade. As we entered, Gregson was telling Hope that until he was called before the magistrates in about a week's time, he would be confined to the hospital, and that anything he might say would be taken down and used in evidence against him.

"Well, that's just fine by me," replied the prisoner. "I've got a great deal to say. I want to tell you gentlemen all about it."

"Hadn't you better reserve that for the trial?" asked Lestrade.

"I may never be tried," he answered. "You needn't look so startled. It isn't suicide I'm thinking off. Are you a doctor?" he asked, turning his dark eyes on me.

"Yes, I am," I replied.

"Then put your hand here," he said, motioning with his manacled wrists towards his chest. I did as instructed and became at once conscious of an extraordinary throbbing and commotion going on inside. The walls of his chest seemed to quiver and quake. Putting my ear to it, I could hear a dull humming and buzzing noise.

"Good heavens!" I cried. "You have an aortic aneurism!"

"That's what they call it," he said calmly. "I went to a doctor a week ago and he told me that I had just a few more days to live. Well, I've done my work now, and I don't care how soon I go, but I should like to leave an account of the business behind me. I don't want to be remembered as a common cut-throat."

Lestrade and Gregson had a hurried discussion about whether he should be allowed to tell his story. "Do you consider, Doctor, that there is immediate danger?" asked Gregson.

"Most certainly there is," I answered.

"In that case it is clearly our duty, in the interests of justice, to take his statement. Jefferson Hope, you are at liberty to give your account," he said, "but I warn you it will be taken down and may be used in evidence against you."

"I'm on the brink of the grave and I'm not likely to lie to you. Every word I say is the absolute truth, and how you use it is a matter of no consequence to me."

With these words, Jefferson Hope began the following remarkable statement. He spoke in a calm and methodical manner, as though the events which he revealed were common enough. I can vouch for the accuracy of the account, for I have had access to Lestrade's notebook in which the prisoner's words were taken down exactly as they were uttered.

"I hated those two men," he said. "It's enough that they were guilty of the death of two human beings — a father and a daughter — and that they had, therefore, forfeited their lives. After

the lapse of time that has passed since their crime, it was impossible for me to secure a conviction against them in any court. I knew of their guilt though, and I determined that I should be judge, jury and executioner all rolled into one. You'd have done the same, if you had been in my place and were man enough.

"My story starts many years ago in the great North American continent. There, in an arid and repulsive desert, two castaways — a man named John Ferrier and a little girl called Lucy — were the sole survivors of a wagon train of settlers making their way west; those not killed by the Indians, died of hunger and thirst. Yet these two survived, though they themselves would have died had they not been found by some other group of travellers. Well, John Ferrier and little Lucy were taken westwards by these people, and settled in the state of Utah. John Ferrier acquired a farm and built a log cabin which received so many additions over the years that it grew into a roomy villa.

"In nine years John Ferrier, through his own hard work, became the most prosperous farmer in the district. And as year succeeded year, little Lucy — whom John Ferrier now adopted as his own daughter — grew taller and stronger so the bud that she was, soon blossomed into a flower.

"One day, when Lucy was by now quite grown up, John Ferrier sent her into Salt Lake

"That was how I first met Lucy, gentlemen. It was I who saved her from almost certain death. It seemed as though it was meant to be. After her thanking me and talking for a while she told me who she was. I knew John Ferrier of old, his name was very familiar to me. My pa and he had been friends in St Louis. So I asked Lucy to remember me to her father when she next saw him. But she did better than that, she invited me to the house. 'He has a lot to thank you for,' she said. 'He's so very fond of me — and so have I.'

"I have never met or seen anyone quite like her before and if the truth be told, I fell in love with her at once. That night I called on old John Ferrier and many times again until my face was a familiar one at the farmhouse. I helped around the place doing odd jobs and working on the land. But one evening after several months had passed, I visited them with some sad news to tell. My partner who owned a silver mine up north had written saying he had struck rich and needed my help for a while. So I had come to tell Lucy that I must leave her, but that when I returned I would claim her as my bride. At this she blushed and laughed and asked what her father would say. I told her straight that I had spoken to him and that he had given his consent. At this she said she was the happiest girl in Utah and begged me not to go. But I had to, and flinging myself onto my horse I galloped furiously away, never once looking back for fear that my determination to go might fail if I took one glance at her."

City on an errand. Now, not only was Miss Lucy beautiful, she was also an accomplished horsewoman. On reaching the outskirts of the city she found the road blocked by a great drove of cattle, driven by six wild-looking herdsmen from the plains. In a matter of seconds she found herself engulfed by a moving stream of fierce-eyed, long-horned bullocks. It was all that she could do to keep herself in the saddle. Just as it seemed that she would fall and be trampled to death a hand caught her frightened horse by the rein and forcing a way through the drove, soon got her to safety.

At this point Jefferson Hope stopped. Turning to me he said, "Give me a glass of water, please. My mouth is dry with all this talking." After pausing for a moment, he then continued. "That was the last I ever saw of Lucy or her father, though I didn't know it at the time.

"The two months came and went, but the work at the silver mine wasn't going as well as expected, so I stayed on. Shortly after this I received a letter from John Ferrier begging me to return as soon as I could. The letter had taken some weeks reaching me, so you can imagine the effect it had on me when I read that John Ferrier had been threatened with eviction from his land if he didn't agree to Lucy marrying Enoch Drebber, one of the biggest and nastiest landowners in all of Utah. Like everyone else I'd always imagined that the land John Ferrier farmed was his own. But it seemed he had only rented it from Drebber's father. When the old man died the son inherited. Now this son was determined to marry Lucy or throw Ferrier off his land.

"I left as soon as I could, but the journey was long and arduous. By the time I reached Salt Lake City it was too late. There I discovered that Drebber and his henchman, Joseph Stangerson, had turned up at Lucy's farm one night and found the place empty. Lucy and her father had just run away. But they hadn't got far before Drebber and Stangerson caught up with them. John Ferrier was shot down in cold blood by Stangerson and Lucy forced back to Salt Lake City. There Drebber married her and there she died shortly afterwards of a broken heart. The terrible death of her father and the effects of the hateful marriage into which she had been forced, meant poor Lucy never held up her head again — but pined away and died within a month.

"From that moment on I vowed that I would avenge the deaths of Lucy and John Ferrier, however long it took me. Before I left, I was given Lucy's wedding-ring by an old woman who had attended her during her illness. The old woman said Lucy would not be buried wearing it. It was the only thing of hers that I had and I kept it with me ever since.

"Drebber and Stangerson soon got to hear that I meant to kill them. I was hounded out of the city and had to flee to the mountains where I hid up for some months and managed, from over-exposure and under-feeding, to get this damned illness.

"Anyway, I could see no way in which I could get even with them, so I returned to the silver mine to make enough money so that one day I would have time enough to meet up with Stangerson and Drebber. I had thought that I would be absent for a year at the most, but a combination of unforeseen circumstances prevented my leaving for nearly five years. Time had not healed the wound. I craved revenge even more strongly than I had on the day when I had stood over poor Lucy's grave.

"I went back to Salt Lake City, but much had changed since last I was there. Drebber and Stangerson had long gone; where, no one knew. They were rich and I was comparatively poor, so it seemed no easy matter to find them. But find them I did after much wandering from town to town through the United States. Year passed into year, but, finally, in Cleveland, Ohio, I just happened to see Drebber's face looking out of a hotel window. He too saw me, and that evening I was arrested by the police on the grounds that Drebber and Stangerson were in danger of their lives from the jealousy and hatred of an old rival — which indeed was true.

"I was detained for several weeks. When at last I was freed, I discovered that they had departed for Europe. Money was again short, so I had to work for a long time before I was able to make the trip to Europe, and continue my search. There they led me a merry dance, always able to keep one step ahead of me: St Petersburg, Copenhagen, Berlin, Paris — I visited them all. Finally I caught up with them in London, by which time my pocket was again empty, and I had to turn my hand to something to make my living. Driving and riding are as natural to me as walking, so I applied at a cab-owner's office, and soon got a job as cabby. I had to bring in a certain amount of money a week to the owner, and whatever was left I could keep for myself. There was seldom much over, but I managed to survive somehow.

"It was some while before I found out where Drebber and Stangerson were staying. But I made inquiries until at last I came across them in a boarding-house in Camberwell, on the south side of the river. I knew then that I had them at my mercy. I would follow them relentlessly until I saw an opportunity. I was determined that they should not escape me, now that I had found them at last. I had no fear that they would recognize me — the years had made sure of that — at least until I wanted them to recognize me.

"Wherever they went in London I was always on their heels. Sometimes I followed them in my cab, sometimes on foot. They were cunning though. They must have thought that there was some chance of their being followed, for they would never go out alone, and never after nightfall. For two weeks I drove behind them in my cab every day, and never once saw them separate. Drebber himself was drunk half the time, but Stangerson was not to be caught napping. I watched them late and early, and never saw the ghost of a chance; but I was not discouraged, for something told me that the hour had almost come. My only fear was that this thing in my chest might burst a little too soon and leave my work undone.

"At last, one evening as I was driving up and down Torquay Terrace, the street in which they boarded, I saw a cab drive up to their door. Presently some luggage was brought out and after a time Drebber and Stangerson followed it, and drove off. I whipped up my horse and kept within sight of them, feeling very ill at ease, for I feared that they were going to change their lodgings. At Euston Station they got out, and leaving a boy to hold my horse, I followed them on to the station platform. I heard them ask for the Liverpool train and the guard answer that one had just gone, and there would not be one for some hours.

"Stangerson seemed to be put out by this, but Drebber seemed pleased. I got so close to them in the bustle that I could hear every word they said. Drebber said that he had a little business of his own to do, and that if

Stangerson would wait, he would soon rejoin him. At this Stangerson seemed to get real angry and said that they had to stick together as agreed. To this Drebber merely said that the business he had was of a delicate nature and that he had to go alone. Stangerson then said something I couldn't catch, but Drebber just swore and cursed and reminded him that he was nothing more than a paid servant, and that what he, Drebber did, was none of Stangerson's business. At this Stangerson gave up and said that if Drebber missed the last train he would find him at Halliday's Private Hotel, to which Drebber answered that he would be back on the platform before eleven, then made his way out of the station.

"The moment for which I had waited so long had come at last. I had my two enemies within my power. Together they could protect each other, but singly they were at my mercy. I did not act hastily. There is no satisfaction in vengeance unless the offender has time to realize who it is that strikes him, and why retribution has come upon him.

"It so happened that some days before, a gentleman who had been looking for some houses in the Brixton Road had dropped the key of one of them in my cab. It was claimed that same evening and returned; but not before I had taken a moulding of it and had a duplicate made. With this key I had access to at least one spot in this great city where I could be free from interruption. How to get Drebber to that house was the difficult problem that I had now to solve.

"When Drebber left the station he walked down the road and went into one or two liquor shops — pubs I think you call them over here — staying for nearly half an hour in the last of them. When he came out, he staggered in his walk, and was evidently pretty drunk. There was a hansom cab just in front of me and he hailed it. I followed it so close that the nose of my horse was within a yard of his driver the whole way. We rattled across Waterloo Bridge and through miles of streets, until, to my astonishment, we found ourselves back in Torquay Terrace. I couldn't imagine why he should return there; but I went on and pulled up my cab a hundred yards or so from the boarding-house. He entered it, and his hansom drove away.

"Give me some more water, please, Doctor, my throat is parched."

Again I gave him the water he asked for and it was some little time before he was able to resume his remarkable testimony.

"Well, I waited a quarter of an hour or so, when suddenly there came a noise like people struggling inside the house. Next moment the door was flung open and two men appeared, one of them was Drebber, and the other was a much younger man whom I had never seen before. This fellow had Drebber by the collar, and when they came to the top of the steps he gave him a shove and a kick which sent him half across the road. 'You keep away from my sister, do you hear!' he shouted, shaking his stick at him. 'You come near her again and I'll give you the thrashing of your life!'

"He was so angry I think he would have killed him, had not Drebber staggered away down the road as fast as his legs would carry him. He ran as far as the corner, and seeing my cab, he hailed me and jumped in. 'Drive me to Halliday's Private Hotel,' he said.

"When I had him safely inside my cab, my heart jumped with joy. I drove along slowly, weighing up what best to do. I thought to take him out into the country and in some deserted lane have my last interview with him. I had almost decided on this, when he solved the problem for me. The craze for drink had seized him again, and he ordered me to pull up outside a pub. He went in, leaving word that I should wait for him. He remained inside until closing

time, and when he came out he was so far gone that I knew the game was in my own hands.

"Don't imagine that I intended to kill him in cold blood. It would only have been just if I had done so, but I could not bring myself to do it. I had long made up my mind that I would give him the chance of saving his own life if he chose to take advantage of it.

"Among the many jobs I had in America during my wandering life, I was once janitor and sweeper-out of the chemical laboratory at York College. One day the professor was lecturing on poisons, and he showed his students some alkaloid, as he called it, which he had extracted from a South American arrow poison, and which was so powerful that to take the smallest grain meant instant death. I spotted the bottle in which this preparation was kept, and when they had all gone, I helped myself to a little of it. I was a fairly good dispenser, so I made this alkaloid into small, soluble pills, and each pill I put in a box with a similar pill made without the poison. I decided that when the chance came, Drebber and Stangerson should each have a draw out of one of these boxes, while I ate the pill that remained. It would be quite as deadly and a good deal less noisy than shooting them with a pistol wrapped in a handkerchief. From that day I had always my pill-boxes with me, and the time had now come when I was to use them.

"It was nearer one o'clock than twelve, and a wild, bleak night it was; very windy and raining in torrents. As I drove, I could see old John

Ferrier and sweet Lucy looking at me out of the darkness and smiling at me, just as plain as I see you all in this room. All the way they were ahead of me, one on each side of the horse, until I pulled up at the house in the Brixton Road.

"There was not a soul to be seen, nor a sound to be heard, except the dripping of the rain. When I looked in at the window of the cab, I found Drebber all huddled in a drunken sleep. I shook him by the arm, 'It's time to get out,' I said. 'All right, cabby,' he replied.

"I guess he thought he had arrived at his hotel, for he got out without another word and followed me down the garden path. I had to walk beside him to keep him steady, for he was still a little unsteady on his feet. When we came to the front door, I opened it, and led the way into a back room at the end of a corridor. I give my word that all the way, the father and the daughter were walking in front of us.

" 'It's infernally dark,' he said, stamping about.

" 'We'll soon have a light,' I said, striking a match and putting it to a wax candle I had brought with me. 'Now, Enoch Drebber,' I said, turning to him, and holding the light to my face, 'who am I?'

"He gazed at me with bleared, drunken eyes for a moment, and then I saw a horror spring up in them, and distort his whole features, which showed me that he recognized me. He staggered back and I saw the perspiration break out on his forehead, while his teeth chattered in his head. Well, I just leaned my back against the door and laughed out loud and long. I had always known that vengeance would be sweet, but I had never hoped for the pleasure which I now enjoyed.

" 'You dog!' I cried, 'I've hunted you down from Salt Lake City to St Petersburg, and you have always escaped me. Now, at last, your wanderings are over, for either you or I shall never see tomorrow's sun.' He shrunk still farther away as I spoke, and I could see on his face that he thought that I was mad. So I was at the time. The pulse in my temples beat like sledge-hammers, and I believe I would have had a fit of some sort if the blood had not, at that moment, suddenly gushed from my nose and relieved me.

" 'What do you think of Lucy Ferrier now?' I shouted, locking the door and waving the key in his face. 'Punishment has been slow in coming, but has caught up with you at last.' I saw his lips tremble as I spoke. He would have begged for his life, but he knew that it was useless.

" 'Would you murder me in cold blood?' he cried.

" 'What mercy did you show when you shot John Ferrier and dragged my Lucy away from her slaughtered father and force her to marry you?'

" 'I didn't kill her father,' he cried, 'It was Stangerson.'

" 'But it was you who broke her heart,' I screamed, thrusting the little pill-box under his nose. 'Let God above judge between us. Choose and eat. There is death in one, and life in the other. I shall take the one you leave. Let us see whether there is any justice on this earth, or if we are ruled by chance.'

"He cowered away with wild cries and screams for mercy, but I drew my knife and held it against his throat until he obeyed me. When he had taken and swallowed one pill, I took the other, and we stood facing each other in silence a minute or more waiting to see which of us was to live, and which to die. I shall never forget the look on his face when the first warning pangs told him that the poison was in his system. I laughed as I saw it, and held Lucy's ring in front of his eyes. It was but for a

moment, for the action of the poison was rapid. A spasm of pain contorted his features; he threw his hands out in front of him, staggered and then, with a hoarse cry, fell heavily on to the floor. I turned him over with my foot, and placed my hand on his heart. There was no movement. He was dead!

"The blood had been streaming from my nose, but I hadn't noticed. I don't know what it was that put it into my head to write on the wall with it. Perhaps it was to put the police on the wrong track, for I felt light-hearted and cheerful. I remembered a German being found in New York with *Rache* written above him. I guessed what puzzled the New Yorkers would puzzle the Londoners, so I dipped my finger in my own blood and wrote on the wall. Then I walked back to my cab and seeing there was no one about, drove off. I had gone some distance when I put my hand in the pocket in which I usually kept Lucy's ring, and found that it wasn't there. I was thunderstruck at this, for it was the only memento that I had of her.

"Thinking that I might have dropped it when I had stooped over Drebber's body, I drove back, and leaving my cab in a side street, I went

boldly up to the house — for I was willing to risk everything rather than lose that ring. But when I arrived, I walked straight into the arms of a police officer who was coming out of the gate. So I pretended to be hopelessly drunk in order to allay his suspicions.

"That was how Enoch Drebber came to his end. All I had to do then was to do as much to Stangerson, and so pay off John Ferrier's death. I knew that he was staying at Halliday's Private Hotel, so I hung about all the next day, but he never came out. I guess he suspected something when Drebber failed to show up. He was cunning, was Stangerson, and always on his guard. If he thought that he could keep me off by staying indoors, he was very much mistaken. I soon found out which was the window of his bedroom, and early next morning I used a ladder I had seen lying in the lane behind the hotel, and so made my way into his room just before it began to get light.

"Stangerson was asleep in bed when I entered, so I woke him up and told him that the hour had come when he was to answer for the life he had taken so long before. I described Drebber's death to him, and gave him the same choice of the poisoned pills. Instead of grasping at the chance of life I offered him, he sprang from his bed and flew at my throat. In self-defence I drew my knife and stabbed him to the heart. It would have been the same in any case, for I am convinced that Providence would never have allowed his guilty hand to pick out anything but the poison pill.

"I've little more to say and it's as well, for I'm about done up. I went on cabbing for a day or two, intending to keep at it until I could save enough to take me back to America. I was standing in the yard when a ragged youngster came up and asked if there was a cabby called Jefferson Hope and if so, his cab was wanted by a gentleman at 221B Baker Street. I went round suspecting nothing, and the next thing I knew, this man here had the bracelets on my wrists. That's the whole of my story, gentlemen. You may think I'm a murderer; but I hold that I'm just as much an officer of justice as you are."

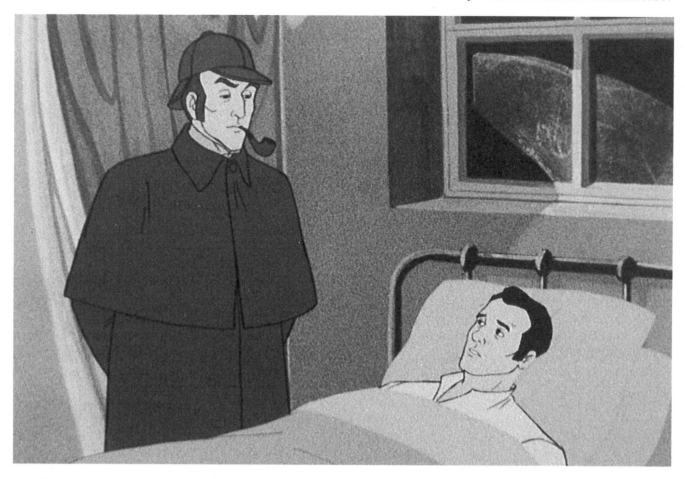

So thrilling had the man's story been and his manner so impressive, that we were all silent and deep in thought for several minutes after he had finished. The only sound was that of Lestrade's pencil scratching the finishing touches to his account.

"There's only one point on which I should like a little more information," Sherlock Holmes said at last. "Who was your accomplice who came for the ring which I advertized?"

The prisoner winked at Holmes. "I can tell my own secrets," he said, "but I don't get other people into trouble. I saw your advert and thought it might be a plant, or might be the ring I wanted. So a friend volunteered to go and see. I think you'll agree he did it smartly."

"No doubt of that," said Holmes heartily.

"Now, gentlemen," Gregson said, gravely, "the law must be complied with. On Thursday the prisoner will be brought before the magistrates, and your attendance will be required. Until then I will be responsible for the prisoner." He rang a bell as he spoke, and two police constables came in to keep watch over Jefferson Hope, while my friend and I took a cab back to Baker Street.

7 The Conclusion

We had been warned to appear before the magistrates on the Thursday; but when the Thursday came there was no need for our testimony. A higher Judge had taken the matter in hand, and Jefferson Hope had been summoned before a tribunal where strict justice would be meted out to him. On the very night after his capture and confession, the aneurism burst and he was found in the morning with a placid smile on his face, as though he had been able in his dying moment to look back on a useful life and on work well done.

"Gregson and Lestrade will be wild about his death," Holmes remarked, as we chatted it over next evening.

"I don't see that they had very much to do with his capture," I answered.

"What you do in this world is a matter of no consequence. The question is what you can make people believe that you have done. Never mind," he added, more brightly, after a pause, "I wouldn't have missed the investigation for anything. There has been no better case within my recollection. Simple as it was, there were several most instructive points about it."

"Simple!"

"Quite so, Watson," said Holmes, smiling at my surprise. "The proof of its simplicity is that without any help save a few very ordinary deductions I was able to lay my hand on the criminal within three days."

"That's true," I said.

"I've already explained to you that what is out of the ordinary is usually a help, rather than a hindrance. In solving a problem of this sort, the ability to reason backwards is a very useful accomplishment. In the everyday affairs of life it is more useful to reason forwards, so the other becomes neglected."

"I confess that I don't quite follow you."

"I hardly expected that you would. Let me see if I can make it clearer. Most people, if you describe a train of events to them, will tell you what the result would be. They can put those

events together in their minds and say that from them something will come to pass. There are few people, however, who, if you told them the *result*, would be able to tell you from thinking alone, what the steps were which led to that result."

"I think I understand," I said.

"Now this was a case in which you were given the result and had to find everything else for yourself. Let me show you the different steps in my reasoning that led me to Jefferson Hope. To begin at the beginning.

"I approached the house, as you know, on foot, and with my mind entirely free of all impressions. I began by examining the roadway, and there, as I have already explained to you, I saw clearly the marks of a cab, which I knew must have been there during the night. I satisfied myself that it was a cab and not a private carriage by the narrow gauge of the wheels. The ordinary London cab is considerably less wide than a gentleman's carriage, you know.

"This was the first point I gained. I then walked slowly down the garden path, which happened to be composed of clay, which is particularly suitable for taking impressions. No doubt it appeared to you to be mere slush, but

to my trained eye every mark on its surface had a meaning — the art of tracing footsteps is a much neglected branch in the science of detection. I, however, was able to see clearly that the heavy footmarks were those of the constable, but I also saw the track of the two men who had first passed through the garden. It was easy to tell that they had been before the others, because in places their marks had been entirely obliterated by other footprints on top of them. In this way my second link was formed, which told me that the visitors in the

night had been two in number, one remarkable for his height (as I calculated from the length of his stride) and the other fashionably dressed, to judge from the small and elegant impression left by his boots.

"On entering the house this was confirmed by the well-booted body lying before me. The tall one, then, had done the murder, if murder there was. There was no wound on the dead man, but the expression on his face told me that he knew of his fate before it came upon him. Men who die from any sudden natural cause never show any sign of agitation on their face. Having sniffed the dead man's lips, I detected a slightly sour smell, and came to the conclusion that he had had poison forced upon him. I knew it had been forced on him by the look of hatred and fear expressed on his face. This was the only conclusion that met all the facts.

"And now came the great question as to the reason why. Robbery was clearly not the motive, for nothing was taken. Was it political assassination, then, or was it a murder committed because of, or for, a woman? I thought from the start that it was most probably over a woman. Political assassins are only too glad to do their work and leave as quickly as possible. This murder had, on the contrary, been done most deliberately, and the murderer had left his tracks all over the room, showing that he had been there all the time. It must have been a private wrong and not a political one, which called for such methodical revenge.

"When the writing was discovered on the wall, I was even more convinced, it was so obviously written to confuse us. And when the ring was found it settled the question. Clearly the murderer had used it to remind his victim of some dead or absent woman. It was at this point that I asked Gregson whether he had inquired in his telegram to Cleveland as to any particular point in Mr Drebber's former career. He answered, you may remember, in the negative.

"I then proceeded to make a careful examination of the room. This confirmed me in my opinion as to the murderer's height and to the length of his nails. I came to the conclusion, since there were no signs of a struggle, that the blood which covered the floor must have burst from the murderer's nose in his excitement. I could see that the track of blood coincided with the track of his feet.

"Having left the house I then proceeded to do what Gregson had neglected to do. I telegraphed to the head of the police in Cleveland, asking for details of the marriage of Enoch Drebber. The answer was conclusive. It told me that Drebber had already applied for the protection of the police against an old rival in love, named Jefferson Hope, and that this Hope was at present in Europe. I knew now that I held the clue to the mystery in my hand, and all that remained to be done was to secure the murderer.

"I had already determined in my own mind that the man who had walked into the house with Drebber was none other than the man who had driven the cab. The marks in the road showed me that the horse had wandered on in a way which would have been impossible had there been anyone in charge of it. Where, then, could the driver be, unless he were inside the house? Secondly, it's absurd to think that any sane man would carry out a deliberate murder under the eyes of a third person, who was sure to betray him. Lastly, supposing a man wished to follow another through London, what better means could he adopt than to turn cabdriver? All these considerations led me to the irresistible conclusion that Jefferson Hope was to be found among the cabmen of London.

"If he had been one, there was no reason to believe that he had ceased to be. From his own point of view, any sudden change would be likely to draw attention to himself. He would probably, for a time at least, continue his duties. And there was no reason to think that he was going under an assumed name. Why should he change his name in a country where no one knew his original one? I therefore organized my street detective corps, and sent them to every cab proprietor in London until they ferreted out the man that I wanted. How well they succeeded, and how quickly I took advantage of it, you know very well. The murder of Stangerson was an incident which was entirely unexpected, but which could hardly in any case have been prevented. Through it, as you know, I came across the pills, the existence of which I had already surmised. You see, my dear Doctor, the whole thing is a chain of logical sequences without a break or a flaw."

"Wonderful, Holmes, wonderful! Your merits should be publicly recognized. You should publish an account of the case. If you won't I'll do it for you."

"You may do as you like, Doctor," he answered. "To the public it is Lestrade and Gregson who solved this case as I said it would be. Take a look at this." It was a newspaper for the day and the paragraph to which Holmes pointed was devoted to the case in question.

'The public,' it said, 'have lost a sensational treat through the sudden death of the man Hope, who was suspected of the murder of Mr Enoch Drebber and of Mr Joseph Stangerson. The details of the case will probably never be known now, though we are informed on good authority that the crime was the result of an old-standing feud, in which love bore a part. It seems that the victims and Hope, the deceased prisoner, hailed from Salt Lake City.

'If the case has no other effect it, at least, brings out in the most striking manner the efficiency of our police force. It is an open secret that the credit of this smart capture belongs entirely to the well-known Scotland Yard detectives, Messrs Lestrade and Gregson. The man was arrested, it appears, in the rooms of Mr Sherlock Holmes, who has himself, as an amateur, shown some talent in the detective line, and who, with such instructors may hope in time to attain some degree of their skill. It is expected that some sort of testimonial will be presented to Lestrade and Gregson as a fitting recognition of their services.'

"Didn't I tell you so?" cried Holmes, with a laugh. "That's the result of all our Study in Scarlet; to get them a testimonial!"

"Never mind," I answered; "I have all the facts written down in my journal and the public shall know of them in time, you may rest assured. Meantime, you must content yourself with the knowledge that without you the Study in Scarlet would forever have remained a mystery."

The Sign of Four

Introduction

HARDLY has Sherlock Holmes finished complaining to Dr Watson about not having any mysteries to solve, when the enchanting Miss Mary Morstan arrives out of the blue to set an intriguing and testing puzzle before him. Soon Holmes and Watson are drawn into a web of clues involving strange gifts, anonymous invitations, "mystery tours", hidden treasure, and murder by the foulest of means. A rapid series of events leads our detectives on an uncanny and exhilarating trail, reaching its climax in a thrilling river chase and a spellbinding piece of storytelling.

We have to thank the American magazine editor and publisher Joseph Stoddard for *The Sign of Four* — and indeed for all the later Holmes stories. After the success of *A Study in Scarlet*, published as a book in 1888, Arthur Conan Doyle was commissioned by Stoddard to write a second Sherlock Holmes story for *Lippincott's Monthly Magazine*. The result was *The Sign of Four*, inspired by Wilkie Collins' haunting novel *The Moonstone*. It was serialized in nine parts in both the American and British editions of the magazine in 1890.

The next year Doyle and his family moved from central London to the leafy suburb of South Norwood — a short cab ride from the sinister Pondicherry Lodge of *The Sign of Four*. There he began his hugely successful series of short stories "starring" Sherlock Holmes and Dr Watson. Only two more full-length Holmes books appeared: *The Hound of the Baskervilles*, in 1901, and *The Valley of Fear*, in 1914.

For those of you who like all the loose ends tied up, Watson *did* marry Mary Morstan, and moved out of 221B Baker Street. After a few happy years Mary died, and Watson moved back to Holmes' famous address.

1 The Statement of the Case

It was a dull afternoon in London and a dense, drizzly fog lay low over the great city. Sherlock Holmes and I had just finished a pleasant lunch, but while I sat reading he paced up and down the room, gazing out the window into the grey street below, then flicking through two or three volumes from the bookcase. Finally he slumped into his favourite chair, and began fiddling with his pipe.

"You seem somewhat restless," I said, rather idly.

"My mind, Watson, rebels at stagnation," he replied, suddenly sitting upright. "Give me problems, give me work, give me the most obscure riddle or cryptic puzzle, and I am in my own proper atmosphere. But I loathe the routine of life. I crave mental stimulation. That's why I have chosen my own particular profession — or rather created it, for I am the only one in the world."

"The only unofficial detective, you mean?" I said, putting aside my book.

"The only unofficial consulting detective," corrected Holmes. "I am the last court of appeal in detection. When Gregson or Lestrade or Athelney Jones are out of their depth — which, by the way, is their normal state — the matter is laid before me. I examine the facts, as an expert, and give a specialist's opinion. I claim no credit in such cases. The work itself, the pleasure of finding a field for my peculiar powers of observation and deduction, is my highest reward."

I was about to press him further on this when, with a crisp knock, our housekeeper entered, carrying a card on the silver salver.

"A young lady to see you, sir," she said, addressing Holmes.

"Miss Mary Morstan," he read. "Hmm. I have no recollection of the name. Ask the young lady to step up, Mrs Hudson."

I rose from my seat to allow my companion to meet his unexpected visitor alone, but he gestured to me to remain seated. "Don't go, doctor," he said kindly. "I should much prefer that you stay."

Miss Morstan entered the room with a firm step and a composed manner. She was a blonde young lady, small, dainty, and dressed in the most perfect taste. There was, however, a plainness and simplicity about her costume which suggested somewhat limited means. Her expression was sweet and amiable, and in an experience of women which extends over three continents and many nations, I have never looked on a face which gave a clearer promise of a refined and sensitive nature. She sat down in the chair Holmes offered her, and placed her bag on her lap.

"I have come to you, Mr Holmes," she began, "because you once helped my employer, Mrs Cecil Forrester, to unravel a domestic complication. She was much impressed both by your skill and by your kindness."

"Mrs Cecil Forrester," he repeated. "I believe I was of some slight service to her. The case, as I recall, was a very simple one."

"She did not think so," replied our visitor. "But at least you cannot say the same of mine. I can hardly imagine anything more strange, more utterly inexplicable, than the situation in which I now find myself."

Holmes rubbed his hands together and leaned forward, an expression of intense concentration on his hawk-like features.

"State your case," said he in brisk, business tones.

I felt that my position was an embarrassing one. "You will, I'm sure, excuse me," I said, rising from my chair.

To my surprise the young lady held up her hand to me. "If your friend would be good enough to remain," she said to Holmes, "he may be of great service to me."

I sat down again on the sofa.

"Briefly, the facts are these," continued Miss Morstan. "My father was an officer in an Indian regiment, and when my mother died he sent me home. I had no relatives here, so I was placed in a comfortable boarding-school in Edinburgh, and there I stayed until I was seventeen. In the year 1878 my father obtained a year's leave and came home. He telephoned me from London to say that he had arrived safely and told me to come down at once to him, giving the Langham Hotel as his address. His message, as I remember, was full of kindness and love."

She paused for a moment, and gave a little fond smile.

"Pray go on," said Holmes.

"On reaching London I drove to the Langham. I was informed that Captain Morstan was staying there, but that he had gone out the night before and not yet returned. I waited all day without news of him and that night, on the advice of the manager, I told the police. The next morning we advertized in all the newspapers, but our inquiries led nowhere, and from that day to this no word has ever been heard of my poor father. He came home with his heart full of hope to find some peace, some comfort, and instead he — he . . ."

She put her handkerchief to her face, and a choking sob cut short the sentence. I got up and put my hand on her shoulder, and asked if I could fetch anything for her. She thanked me for my concern, and apologized for her tears.

"The date, Miss Morstan?" asked Holmes, opening his notebook.

"My father disappeared on the third of December, 1878 — nearly ten years ago."

"And his luggage?"

"It remained at the hotel. There was nothing in it to suggest a clue — some clothes, a few books, and a number of curiosities from the Andaman Islands, where he had been one of the senior officers in charge of the penal settlement."

"Did he have any friends in London?" asked Holmes, taking out his pipe.

"Only one that we know of — Major Sholto, of the same regiment. He retired some little time before my father and lived in Upper Norwood. We contacted him, of course, but he didn't even know that my father was back in England."

"A strange case," remarked Holmes.

"You have yet to hear the strangest part, Mr Holmes," continued Miss Morstan. "About six years ago — on the fourth of May, 1882, to be exact — an advertisement appeared in *The Times* asking for the address of Miss Mary Morstan, and stating it would be to her advantage to come forward. There was no address or name supplied. I had by then entered the family of Mrs Forrester as governess, and on her advice I published my address in the same column of the newspaper. The very same day there arrived through the post a small cardboard box addressed to me, which contained a large and lustrous pearl. No word of writing was enclosed.

"Since then, every year on the same date, a similar box has arrived, containing a similar pearl, each time without any clue as to the identity of the sender. They are of rare quality and considerable value. You can see for yourselves that they are very handsome."

As she spoke she opened a small box and showed me six of the finest pearls I had ever seen. I passed them to my companion.

"Your statement is most interesting," said Holmes, inspecting the pearls. "Has anything else happened to you?"

"Yes, and no later than today. That's why I have come to see you. This morning I received this note."

"Thank you," said Holmes, taking the note passed to him. "The envelope, too, please. Postmark: London, South-West. Date: October 7. Hmm. A man's thumb-mark on corner — probably postman's. Best quality paper and envelope. No address. '*Be at the third pillar from the left outside the Lyceum Theatre tonight at seven o'clock. If you are distrustful bring two friends. You are a wronged woman and shall have justice.*

Do not bring police. If you do, all will be in vain. Your unknown friend.' Well, this is a pretty little mystery! What do you intend to do, Miss Morstan?"

"That's exactly what I want to ask you," she replied, slightly surprised by the question.

"Then we shall most certainly go; you and I and — yes, Dr Watson is the very man. Your correspondent says two friends. He and I have worked together before."

"You are both very kind," she answered. "I have led a sheltered life and have no real friends to whom I could appeal in a situation like this. Shall I come here, then — say at six o'clock?"

"You must be no later," said Holmes. "Pray allow me to keep the papers. It is only half past three, and I may look into the matter before then. Goodbye."

"Goodbye, and thank you," said our visitor; and with a bright, kindly glance from one to the other of us, she replaced her pearl-box in her bag and left.

Standing at the window, I watched her walk briskly down the street until she was but a speck in the sombre crowd. "What a very attractive woman!" I exclaimed, turning round to my companion.

He had lit his pipe again and was sitting back in his chair, gazing at the ceiling. "Is she?" he said languidly. "I can't say I really noticed."

2   In Quest of a Solution

Holmes went out at four o'clock and returned only a few minutes before Miss Morstan's cab arrived punctually at six. He was eager and in excellent spirits, but before we left he took out his revolver from his drawer and slipped it into his pocket. It was obvious he thought our night's work might be a serious one.

Miss Morstan's sensitive face was composed but pale. She must have felt some uneasiness at the strange enterprise on which we were embarking — I must confess that I did — yet her self-control was admirable, and she listened closely to what my companion had to say as the four-wheeled cab made its way across central London to the Lyceum Theatre.

"I have found out on consulting the files of *The Times*," stated Holmes, "that Major John Sholto, of Upper Norwood, late of the Thirty-fourth Bombay Infantry, died on the twenty-eighth of April, 1882."

"I'm sorry, Holmes," I said after a little thought, "but I fail to see the significance of that particular fact."

"No? You surprise me, Watson. Look at it this way, then. Captain Morstan disappears. The only friend in London he could have visited is Major Sholto, who denies having known that he was back in England. Four years later Sholto dies, and within a week of his death — on the fourth of May, 1882, to be precise — Miss Morstan receives a valuable present, which is repeated every year. Why should the presents begin right after Sholto's death unless it is the case that Sholto's heir knows something of the mystery and wants to make amends?"

"But what strange amends!" I said. "And how

strangely done! And why should he write a letter now, rather than six years ago?"

"There are difficulties," replied Holmes. "There are certainly difficulties. But our expedition tonight will solve them all. Now tell me, Miss Morstan, what do you know of the relationship between Sholto and your father?"

"Major Sholto was a particular friend of Papa's," she replied. "His letters often mentioned him. He and Papa were in command of the troops on the Andaman Islands, so they spent much time together. But I don't know any details about him. By the way, Mr Holmes, a curious paper was found in Papa's desk which no-one could understand. I don't suppose that it's of the slightest importance, but I thought you might care to see it, so I brought it with me."

She handed the paper to Holmes, who unfolded it carefully. He then examined it closely with his magnifying glass.

"It is paper of native Indian manufacture," he remarked. "At some time it has been pinned to a board. The diagram on it appears to be a plan of a large building with numerous halls, corridors and passages. At one point is a small cross in red ink, and above it is written '3.37 from left' in faded pencil. In the left-hand corner is a strange drawing like four crosses in a line with their arms touching. Beside this, in very rough characters, is written *'The sign of four — Jonathan Small, Mahomet Singh, Abdullah Khan, Dost Akbar.'* No, I confess that I do not see how this bears upon the matter in hand. Yet it is evidently a document of importance; it has been kept carefully in a pocket-book, for one side is as clean as the other."

"It was in my father's pocket-book that we found it," said Miss Morstan.

"Then preserve it carefully," said Holmes, folding it up and handing it back to her, "for it may prove to be of use to us. I begin to suspect that this matter may turn out to be much deeper and more subtle than I had at first supposed."

Down the Strand the lamps were but misty splotches of light throwing out a feeble glimmer in the fog, and as we stood at our appointed place outside the Lyceum Theatre, waiting for someone to approach us, I began to feel nervous about our weird quest. We had been there only a few minutes, however, when Miss Morstan was addressed by a short man sporting a large moustache and wearing a tall bowler hat.

"Excuse me, miss," he said in a rough, throaty voice, "but are you Miss Morstan?"

"I am," she replied, "and these two gentlemen are my friends."

He bent his gaze upon us, first on Holmes and then on myself. "Forgive me for asking, miss, but I was to ask you to give me your word that neither of your companions is a police officer."

"I give you my word," she answered.

He looked at us again, nodded, and turned away. He put his fingers to his mouth and gave a shrill whistle, a sound which brought a street boy and a coach up to us. He opened the door for us, and after we had stepped in he mounted the driver's seat. We had hardly sat down before he whipped up his horse and we plunged away at a furious pace through the foggy streets.

At first I had some idea as to the direction in which we were driving; but soon, what with our speed, the fog, and my limited knowledge of London, I lost my bearings and knew nothing except that we seemed to be going a very long way. Holmes, by contrast, was never at fault, and he muttered the names as the coach rattled through squares and in and out of tortuous back streets.

"We are making for the other side of the river, apparently," he suddenly said out loud. "Yes, I thought so. We are now on the bridge. You can catch glimpses of the water."

We did manage a fleeting view of a stretch of the Thames, but our coach dashed on and was soon involved in a maze of streets on the south side of the river.

Once again Holmes kept track of our route. "Our quest does not appear to take us to very fashionable districts," he said, and we had indeed now entered a somewhat forbidding neighbourhood. At last the coach drew up at the third house in a new brick terrace. None of the other houses were lived in, and the one outside which we stopped was almost as dark as the others, save for a single glimmer of light from a downstairs window.

The driver opened the door of the coach, then gestured for us to go up the steps to the front door. He unlocked it to let us in, and we then followed him down a dark passage lined with all kinds of ornaments and artifacts from the East, until he came to a door on the left. He knocked on it and stood back in the passage. "Your visitors have arrived, Mr Sholto," he said.

"Thank you, Williams," replied a thin, high voice from inside — and we waited for the appearance of the man who had invited us to this mysterious meeting.

3 The Story of the Bald-headed Man

Williams was joined by a small, thin man, his head bald save for a bristle of red hair all round the base and a tuft of red hair on the top. In spite of his baldness he gave the impression of youth, and in point of fact, as we later discovered, he had just turned his thirtieth year.

"Your servant, Miss Morstan," he said in his little voice, bowing slightly. "Your servant, gentlemen. Pray step into my little sanctum. A small place, but furnished to my own liking, and an oasis of art in the tasteless desert of South London."

It was indeed an impressive room for so drab a house in so dull a district. The richest and heaviest of curtains and tapestries draped the windows and walls, looped back here and there to expose some mounted painting or Oriental vase. The carpet was so soft and thick that the foot sank easily into it, as into a bed of moss. Two great tiger-skins and huge tropical plants in massive pots enhanced the suggestion of Eastern luxury, as did the subtle and aromatic odours wafting from a silver lamp hung from the ceiling.

"Mr Thaddeus Sholto," said the little man. "That is my name. You are Miss Morstan, of course, and these gentlemen —"

"This is Mr Sherlock Holmes," explained our companion, "and this is his friend Dr Watson."

"A doctor, eh?" he cried excitedly, putting his hand on his chest. "Have you your stethoscope with you? Would you have the kindness? I have grave doubts about one of the valves in my heart, if you would be so good."

I listened to his heart, as requested, but could find nothing wrong — except that he was extremely nervous.

"It appears to be normal," I said. "You have no cause for concern."

"I'm delighted and relieved to hear it," replied the little man, smiling. "Had your father not thrown a strain on his heart, Miss Morstan, he might have been alive today."

I could have struck the man across his face, so annoyed was I at this cruel and casual reference to such a delicate matter. Miss Morstan sat down on the settee, her face white and her lip trembling.

"I knew in my heart that he was dead," she said, stifling her tears. "But I always had a lingering hope for some sort of miracle. Tell me, Mr Sholto, how did he die — and what is all this about?"

"I will tell you everything I know," he replied, "and what's more, I will do you justice, whatever my twin brother Bartholomew may say. He's very angry with me for taking the course which has seemed correct to me, and we had quite heated words last night. We four can now show a bold front to Brother Bartholomew, but let us have no outsiders; no police or officials. We can settle everything among ourselves without any interference."

"For my part," said Holmes, "whatever you may choose to tell us will go no further."

I nodded my agreement.

"That is well!" said he. "That is very well! May I offer you a glass of Chianti?"

We all accepted, and after he had poured out the wine he began to tell his tale.

"In the first place," he said, sitting down on the settee next to Miss Morstan, "I must tell you that there are several points of which I am myself ignorant. I can therefore only lay the facts before

you as far as I know them."

"Please do so," said Holmes, getting out his notebook and pencil.

"My father was, as you may have guessed, Major John Sholto, once of the Indian Army. He retired some eleven years ago and came to live in London, at Pondicherry Lodge in Norwood. I well remember the sensation caused by the disappearance of Captain Morstan the following year. My father joined in the speculation as to what could have happened — but never for one moment did we suspect that he had the whole secret locked away in his heart; that of all men, only he knew the fate of Arthur Morstan.

"We did know, however, that some mystery, some sort of danger, hung over our father, though he would never tell us what it was. He was fearful of going out alone, and he always employed two former prize-fighters at Pondicherry Lodge. Williams, who drove you here tonight, was one of them. Once he fired his revolver at a man with a wooden leg who turned out to be a harmless tradesman, and we had to

pay a large sum of money to hush the matter up.

"Then, early in 1882, my father received a letter from India which was a great shock to him, and from that day he quickly sickened to his death. We never could discover what was in this letter, but he became rapidly worse and, in the April of that year, he was told he had only days to live. He called us to him and said he had something of vital importance to tell us. He told us of the treasure — the Agra treasure, he called it — which he had chanced on in India and brought home to England. He said that the only thing that still weighed on his mind was his treatment of Miss Morstan. After he had passed on, we were to make sure she received her fair share of the treasure. He explained that ten years ago your father, Miss Morstan, came home to retire and, on his first night in London, went to Norwood to claim his share of the jewels."

Sholto paused for a moment, giving Miss Morstan a sympathetic look. "An argument developed between the two men as to how the treasure should be divided; your father, wild

have thought that our imaginations had conjured up that face. But we soon had more striking proof, for in the morning the door to my father's room was open. His drawers and cupboards had been disturbed, and on his chest was a torn piece of paper with the words '*The sign of four*' scrawled across it. What the phrase meant or who our secret visitor may have been, we never knew. As far as we could tell, nothing of my father's property had actually been stolen."

The little man now stood up, one hand resting on the arm of the settee. We had all sat absorbed in listening to his extraordinary tale, and now, as I glanced at Holmes leaning back thoughtfully in his chair, I could not help thinking of how on this very day he had complained bitterly about the dull routine of life. Here, surely, was a problem that would test his skills to the utmost.

Thaddeus Sholto looked down at each of us, obviously proud at the effect his story had produced. "My brother and I were, as you can well imagine, much excited about the treasure. For weeks — months — we dug and delved in every part of the grounds without discovering even a clue to its whereabouts. We could judge the splendour of the missing riches by the pearls he had taken out.

"My brother and I had some little discussion about these pearls. They were obviously of value, and he was averse to part with them — between us, as friends, he was somewhat inclined towards my father's great fault. He thought, too,

with anger, had a heart attack and collapsed, hitting his head on the corner on the chest. My father was terrified that he would be accused of murder and so, helped by his trusted servant Lal Chowdar — who himself died shortly afterwards — disposed of the body that very night. A few days later the papers were full of the mysterious disappearance of Captain Morstan.

"At this point my father, growing weaker with every word, called us closer to him. 'Listen carefully to me,' he whispered, 'the treasure is hidden . . .' At this exact moment a ghastly change came over his pale face; his eyes stared wildly to the side, his jaw dropped, and he raised his hands up in front of him, yelling out, 'Keep him away! For God's sake keep him away!' We both stared round at the window on which his gaze had been fixed. A face was peering in at us out of the darkness — a bearded face with fierce, cruel eyes. My brother and I rushed to the window, but the face was gone. When we returned to my father his head had dropped and his heart had stopped beating.

"We searched the garden for the intruder but found no sign of him — none except that, under the window, there was a single footmark visible in the flower-bed. But for that one trace, we may

that if we parted with them it might eventually bring us into trouble. It was all I could do to persuade him to let me find out Miss Morstan's address and send her a detached pearl every year so that at least she would never be destitute."

"It was a kind thought," said Miss Morstan earnestly. "It was extremely good of you."

The little man put both hands on the arm of the settee and leaned towards our companion. "We were your trustees," he explained. "That's the way I saw the matter. We had plenty of money, and it would have been bad taste to treat a lady in so dishonest a fashion. But Brother Bartholomew did not see it in that light, and our difference of opinion grew so strong that I felt the need to move away from the Lodge, taking Williams with me."

"And what has happened to produce this invitation here tonight?" asked Holmes.

"Yesterday an event of extreme importance occurred. The treasure was discovered! I instantly communicated with Miss Morstan, and it only remains for us to drive to Norwood and demand our share. I explained my views last night to Brother Bartholomew, so we shall be expected, if not welcome, visitors."

We all sat for a moment, taking in this new development, then Holmes sprang to his feet. "You have done well, sir, from first to last," said he. "It is possible that we may be able to repay you in some small measure by throwing some light on that which is still dark to you. But it is late, and we had best put the matter through without delay."

Our coach was waiting outside, and Williams again took off at a rapid pace, Thaddeus Sholto talking incessantly in a voice which rose high above the rattle of the wheels.

"Bartholomew is a clever fellow," he said, addressing Holmes. "He had come to the conclusion that the treasure was somewhere inside the house, so he worked out all the measurements. He found that the height of the building was seventy-eight feet, but that on adding together all the heights of the separate rooms, and allowing for the space between, and estimating the depth underneath by borings, he could not get more than seventy feet. That left eight feet unaccounted for.

"These could only be at the top of the building. So, last evening, he and I knocked a hole in the ceiling above the highest room and there; sure enough, we came upon a little garret

71

above it; it had been sealed up and was known to no-one. In the centre stood the treasure-chest. I helped him lower it through the hole, and there it lies. He reckons the value of the jewels at not less than half a million pounds."

At the mention of this gigantic sum we all stared at each other, open-mouthed. Even Holmes, whom I have never seen at a loss, was staggered. If her rights were secured, Miss Morstan would change from a governess to the richest heiress in the land.

It was the place of any friend to rejoice at the news, but I'm ashamed to admit that selfishness took me by the soul and turned as heavy as lead within me. I stammered out a few halting words of congratulation but then sat downcast, deaf to the babble of our new acquaintance. How could I, a retired army surgeon with a weak leg and a weaker bank account, dare now to think of attracting the affections of a young, pretty woman who would become the richest female in England?

I was jolted from my maudlin thoughts by our coach coming to a sudden halt, and Williams climbing down to open the door.

"This, Miss Morstan, is Pondicherry Lodge," said Thaddeus Sholto as he handed her out on to the driveway.

4 The Tragedy of Pondicherry Lodge

It was nearly eleven o'clock when we reached this stage of our night's adventures. We had left the damp fog of the city behind us, and the night was fairly fine. Clouds skudded across the sky, a nearly full moon now and again peeping through them.

Pondicherry Lodge was a huge clump of a house, plunged in shadow except for the light from two windows. The vast size of the building, with its gloom and its deathly silence, struck a chill to the heart. Even Thaddeus Sholto seemed ill at ease as he led us to the great front door.

We had gone only a few steps, however, when the door opened and a stout woman came running from the house towards us.

"It's Mrs Bernstone, the housekeeper," said Sholto. "Something is obviously wrong!"

"Oh, thank heavens you've come, Mr Thaddeus!" she panted, holding her head in her hands. "It's your brother, sir! He's locked himself in his room and neither me nor his Indian servants can get a word out of him. You must go up, Mr Thaddeus. I can tell he must be ill!"

Thaddeus Sholto was now quaking with fear, and began blubbering about his nerves and his heart.

"Direct us to the room," ordered Holmes, brushing past the frozen figure of Sholto. "There may be no time to lose!"

I followed the poor woman and Holmes into the house and up first one flight of stairs and then another, glancing back at the top to see that Miss Morstan was coaxing the reluctant Sholto into the hall. Mrs Bernstone went down a corridor on the second floor and stopped outside the third door on the left.

Holmes knocked hard, but there was no

answer. Then he turned the handle and tried to force it open. It was locked on the inside, however, by a broad and strong bolt, as we could see when we put a lantern up against the door. With the key turned, the hole was not entirely closed, and Holmes stooped to look through.

"There is something devilish in this, Watson," he said as he stood upright. "What do you make of that?"

I bent down to the hole — and was amazed by what I saw. There was the figure of a man — for all the world the head of our new acquaintance — slumped over a bench or table.

"This is terrible!" I said to Holmes, "What do we do now?"

"The door must come down!" he answered. "Come on, Watson!"

Together we flung ourselves against it; it creaked and groaned, but did not yield. We tried again, with the same result. The third time, however, it gave way with a sudden snap, and we found ourselves in Bartholomew Sholto's strange room.

It was fitted up as a chemical laboratory, and was littered with glass bottles, Bunsen burners and test-tubes. One large bottle appeared to have been broken, for a stream of dark liquid had trickled from it, and the air was heavy with a tar-like odour. A set of steps stood towards one side of the room in a mess of lath and plaster, and above them was a large hole in the ceiling.

The master of the house was seated all in a heap, his head sunk on the table. Pinned to his clothes was a piece of paper with some words scrawled on it. Holmes took it off the body, glanced at it, and handed it to me.

"You see, Watson," he said confidently.

In the light of the lantern I read, with a thrill of horror, 'The Sign of Four'.

"In God's name what does it all mean?" I asked.

"It means murder," said he, poised over the dead man. "Ah, I expected it. Look here!"

He pointed to what looked like a dark thorn stuck in the skin of the neck, just below the ear.

"It looks like a thorn," I said.

"It is a thorn. You may pick it out. But be careful — it is poisoned!"

I took the dreadful thing between my finger and thumb. It came away from the skin so readily that hardly any mark was left behind, and only a tiny speck of blood showed where the puncture had been.

"This is all a mystery to me," I said. "It grows darker instead of clearer."

"On the contrary, Watson," replied Holmes airily, "it clears every minute. I only require a few missing links to have an entirely connected case."

We had almost forgotten the other parties involved since we entered the room. Sholto was now standing in the doorway, the very picture of fear, wringing his hands and moaning to himself. Suddenly, however, he let out a sharp cry.

"The treasure's gone!" he said. "They've robbed him of the treasure! I helped him lower it through that hole last night. I was the last person who saw him! I left him here, and I heard him lock the door behind me!"

"What time was that, Mr Sholto?" asked Holmes, polite but firm.

"About ten o'clock. And now he's dead, and I'll be suspected of having a hand in it. But you don't think it was me, gentlemen, do you? I wouldn't have brought you here if it were me, would I? Oh dear, oh dear! I think I will go mad!"

"You have no reason for fear," said Holmes. "Take my advice, Mr Sholto, and drive down to the station with Williams to report the matter to the police. Offer to assist them in every way you can. We shall wait here until your return."

The little man, clearly more worried than bereaved about the death of his twin brother, brushed past Miss Morstan and Mrs Bernstone and disappeared down the hallway.

"Miss Morstan," continued Holmes, "would you be so kind as to have this good woman show you the way to her room. She has had an unpleasant shock, and I suggest you stay with her until we leave."

"Of course, Mr Holmes," replied Miss Morstan. "I'm glad to be of any assistance in this dreadful business."

We had all had shocking experiences that evening, not least Miss Morstan herself, and my admiration for her grew still further as she guided the sobbing housekeeper from that cold chamber of death.

5 Holmes Gives a Demonstration

"Now Watson," said Holmes, rubbing his hands together in anticipation, "we have half an hour to ourselves. Let us make good use of it. My case is, as I have told you, almost complete, but we must not err towards over-confidence. Simple as the matter seems now, there may be something deeper underlying it."

"Simple!" I cried.

"Surely," said he, with something of the air of a professor expounding to his young class. "Just stand over there, so that your footprints do not complicate the issue. Now, to work!"

He stood still for a moment, surveying the room. "In the first place, how did these folk come in and how did they leave? The door has not been opened since last night. But what of the window?"

He carried the lantern across to it, muttering his observations aloud but addressing them to himself rather than to me. "Window is locked on the inside. Framework is solid. No hinges at the side. Let us open it. Hmm — no water-pipe near. Roof quite out of reach. Yet a man has entered by the window. It rained a little early last night, and there is the print of a foot in mould on the sill. And here on the floor a circular muddy mark . . . and another . . . and another by here by the table. See here, Watson! This really is a very pretty clue!"

"I looked at the round, well-defined discs. "They're no footprints," I said.

"They are something far more valuable to us, good doctor. They are the impressions of a stump."

"Good heavens! You mean a man with a wooden leg!"

"Quite so, Watson. But there has been someone else — a very able and efficient ally. Could you scale that wall?"

I looked out of the open window. The moon still shone brightly on that part of the house. We were a good fifty feet from the ground and, look where I would, I could see no foothold, not even a crevice in the brickwork. "It's absolutely impossible," I answered.

"Without help it is," said Holmes. "But suppose you had a friend up here, who lowered you that good stout rope in the corner there,

securing one end of it to this great hook in the wall. Then, I think, if you were a reasonably active man, you might clamber up, wooden leg and all. You would depart in the same way, and your ally would draw up the rope, untie the hook, shut the window, lock it from the inside, and leave the way he came.

"This is all very well," said I, "but the thing becomes more puzzling by the moment. What about this mysterious ally? How did he get into the room?"

"Ah yes, the strange ally!" repeated Holmes excitedly. There are interesting features about him. He lifts the case from the ordinary, and I fancy he breaks fresh ground in the annals of British crime."

"How then did he get in?" I reiterated. "The door was locked and bolted, the window out of reach."

"How often have I said to you, Watson," he answered, shaking his head, "that when you have eliminated the impossible, whatever remains, however unlikely it may seem, must be the truth? We know that he did not come through the door, or the window, and we also know that he could not have concealed himself in the room, for no concealment is possible. How then, did he come?"

"He came through the hole in the roof!" I cried, relieved at solving the problem.

"Quite so. He must have done. If you will have the kindness to hold the lantern for me, we will now extend our searches to the room above — the secret room in which the treasure was found."

He mounted the steps and, pausing to study the sad figure of Bartholomew Sholto, pulled himself up into the garret above. He reached down for the lantern, and I climbed up after him. The accumulated dust of years lay on the floor.

"Here you are," said Holmes, putting his hand against the sloping wall. "This skylight leads out on to the roof. This, then, is the route by which Number One entered the house."

He closed the skylight and held the lantern down to the floor. It was covered with the clear prints of naked feet — perfectly formed, but barely half the size of those of a normal man.

"Holmes," I said in a whisper, "a child has done this horrid thing!"

"Not a child, Watson, not a child. But notice how the print of each toe is separate and distinct, not cramped up to the next. These are the prints of feet which have never worn shoes or boots. That is the point. I was, I confess, thrown for the moment, but the thing is quite natural. My memory failed me, or I should have been able to foretell it. But let us go down; there is nothing more to be learned here."

"What is your theory, then, as to those foot-marks?" I asked eagerly when we had returned to Sholto's room.

"My dear Watson, try a little analysis yourself," he replied with a touch of impatience. "You know my methods. Apply them."

"I cannot conceive of anything which will cover all the facts," I answered lamely.

"It will be clear enough to you soon," he said in an offhand way. "I think there is nothing else of importance here, but I will look."

He took out his glass and a small tape measure and went about the room on his knees — measuring, comparing, examining, his long thin nose only inches from the planks, his beady eyes darting like those of a bird of prey. So swift and silent and furtive were his movements that I could not but think what a master criminal he would have made had he turned his energy and skills against the law instead of exerting them in its defence. As he hunted about, he kept muttering to himself, until he finally broke out into a loud crow of delight.

"We are in luck, Watson! We will have very little trouble now. Number One has had the misfortune to tread in the creosote from the broken bottle. You can see the outline of the edge of his small foot here, at the side of this evil-smelling mess. I know a dog that would follow that scent to the very end of the world!"

Just then we heard a coach pull up outside, and the sound of loud voices.

"That will be Sholto and the police," said Holmes. "Before they come, good doctor, just put your hand on this poor fellow's arm, and here, on his leg. What do you feel?"

"The muscles are as hard as a board," I answered.

"Quite so. They are in a state of extreme contraction, far exceeding the usual *rigor mortis* that sets in after death. Along with the distortion of the face, what does that suggest to you?"

"Death from some powerful vegetable substance," I offered, "some strychnine-like poison which would produce tetanus."

"That is exactly what occurred to me the instant I saw the tight, drawn muscles of the face. Do you have the thorn?"

I took it out and held it in the light of the lantern. It was long, sharp and black, glazed near the point as though some gummy substance had dried on it. The blunt end had been trimmed and rounded off with a knife.

"Is that an English thorn?" he asked.

"No, it certainly isn't."

"Then with all this data you should be able to draw some conclusions, Watson. But enough for the moment — here are the forces of the law."

As he spoke a very large, portly man strode heavily down the hallway and stood inside the door of the room. He was heavy-jowled, with a pair of small eyes which peered out from the top of his pear-shaped face. He was closely followed by the petrified figure of Thaddeus Sholto.

"Here's a business, then!" cried the police-man in a muffled, husky voice. "Here's a pretty business! But who are all these. The house seems to be as full as a rabbit warren!"

"Good evening, Mr Athelney Jones," said Holmes. "I think you must remember me."

"Why, if it isn't Mr Sherlock Holmes, the theorist," he wheezed. "Remember you? I'll never forget how you lectured us all on the Bishopsgate jewel case. You set us on the right track, I'll grant you, but you'll own up now that it was more by good luck than good guidance."

"It was a piece of very simple reasoning, Superintendent."

"Oh come now, Mr Holmes! Never be

ashamed to own up. But what's all this? Bad business! Bad business! Grim facts here — no room for fancy theories. How lucky that I happened to be out at Norwood on another case! I was at the station when Mr Sholto arrived. What do you reckon the man died of?"

"Oh, this is hardly a case for me to theorize about, Superintendent," replied Holmes dryly.

"No, no, quite right," said the Superintendent. "Still, we can't deny that you hit the nail on the head sometimes. Dear me — door locked, I understand. Jewels worth half a million gone missing. What about the window?"

"Fastened," said Holmes, "but there are footprints on the sill."

"Well, if it was fastened the prints could have nothing to do with the matter — that's common sense. The man may have died in a fit. Ah, I have a theory! These flashes come on me sometimes. Just step outside, please, Mr Sholto, and join the sergeant at the end of the hallway. Er, your friend can remain, Mr Holmes, of course."

"Thank you," replied Holmes. "My friend's name is Doctor John Watson."

"Pleased to make your acquaintance, Doctor Watson. Now, Holmes, what do you think of this? Sholto, by his own admission, was with his brother last night. The brother had a fit, and Sholto walked off with the treasure."

"And the dead man very considerately got up and locked the door on the inside," said Holmes.

"Hmm, there is a flaw there. But this Thaddeus Sholto was with his brother. The brother is dead and the jewels are gone. No-one saw the brother from the time Thaddeus left him, and his bed has not been slept in. Sholto is obviously in a most disturbed state. The net begins to close upon Thaddeus Sholto."

"You are not quite in possession of all the facts yet," said Holmes. "This splinter of wood, which I have every reason to believe was poisoned, was in the dead man's neck; and this card, inscribed as you see, was on the body. How do those facts fit into your theory?"

"Confirms it in every respect," said the fat detective pompously. "House is full of Indian

curiosities, and the card is some hocus-pocus or other — a blind, as like as not. The only question is, how did the murderer get in and out? Ah, of course, there's a hole in the ceiling."

With great agility, considering his bulk, he sprang up the steps and lifted himself into the garret. We heard the thud of his head hitting a rafter, followed by a deadened voice: "I knew it! There's a skylight up here."

"He can find something," said Holmes to me quietly. "He has occasional glimmerings of reason."

"You see!" cried Jones, reappearing on the steps. "Facts are better than theories. There's a skylight on to the roof, partly open."

"It was I who opened it," said Holmes.

"Oh, you noticed it, then? Well, whoever noticed it, it shows how our man got away. Sergeant!"

"Yes, sir!" came the cry from the hallway.

"Ask Mr Sholto to step this way."

Jones looked fairly pleased with himself as the sergeant led in a terrified, quaking Thaddeus Sholto.

"Mr Thaddeus Sholto," began Jones, "I arrest you in the name of the Queen as being concerned in the death of your brother. It is my duty to inform you that anything you say may be used against you . . ."

"No, no!" cried Sholto, turning to Holmes. "I told you. I told you they would suspect me! It's all a terrible mistake!"

"Don't trouble yourself about it, Mr Sholto," said Holmes calmly. "I think I can clear you of the charge."

"Don't promise too much, Holmes!" snapped the detective. "You may find it harder than you think."

Holmes began to fill his pipe with tobacco. "Not only will I clear him, Mr Jones, but I will now make a present of the name and description of one of the two people who were in this room with Bartholomew Sholto last night. His name is Jonathan Small, a small, active, middle-aged man with his left leg off, and wearing a wooden stump which is worn on the inner side. His boot has a square-toed sole, with a metal band round the heel. He is probably bearded. These few incidental clues, coupled with the fact that he was once a convict, may be of some assistance to you. The other man —"

"Ah, yes, the other man!" said Athelney Jones in a sneering voice, though obviously impressed nevertheless.

" — is a rather curious person," continued Holmes, heading towards the door. "I hope before very long to introduce you to the pair of them. A word with you, Watson."

He led me out past the open-mouthed detective and up the hallway.

"This unexpected event has caused us to lose sight of the original purpose of our journey," he said.

"I've just been thinking the same thing myself," I answered. "It's not right that Miss Morstan should remain any longer in this stricken house."

"Quite. You must escort her home, using Williams and Sholto's four-wheeler. She lives with Mrs Forrester in Camberwell, so it is not too far. I will wait for you here if you will drive out again — or perhaps you are too tired?"

"By no means, Holmes. I don't think I could sleep a wink until I know more of this fantastic business. I should like to see the matter through with you, now that I've got so far."

"Good man," he answered. "Your presence will be of great service to me. We shall work the case out for ourselves and leave this fellow Jones to follow his own devices. When you have left Miss Morstan, I wish you to go on to Pinchin Lane, down near the water's edge at Lambeth. The second house on the right-hand side, number three, is the home of a bird-stuffer called Sherman; get him up and tell him, with my compliments, that I want Toby at once. You will bring Toby back here with you."

"A dog, I suppose?" I said.

"Yes, a queer mongrel with the most amazing power of scent. I would rather have Toby's help at this point than the whole detective force of London."

"I shall bring him, then," said I, getting into the coach. "It's now nearly two o'clock. I ought to be back around four."

"And I," said Holmes, "shall see what I can learn from Mrs Bernstone and from the Indian servant. Thaddeus tells me he sleeps in the very next room. Then I shall study the great Jones' methods and listen to his words of wisdom."

6 On the Trail of the Murderers

Until now Miss Morstan had borne the troubles of the night with great fortitude; but now, in the coach, she began weeping, and my heart went out to her. Yet there were two thoughts that prevented my showing my feelings. First, she was weak and helpless, and it was to take her at a disadvantage to state my affections at such a time. Worse still, she would soon be rich, and perhaps she would see my actions as those of a vulgar fortune-seeker. The treasure intervened like an impassable barrier between us.

It was nearly two o'clock when we reached Mrs Forrester's house. Her servants had retired to bed hours before, but she was so intrigued by the message of the previous evening that she had waited up for her governess. I discharged my duties and left for Pinchin Lane, a row of shabby, two-storeyed houses in the lower quarter of Lambeth. I had to knock some time at number three, but at last the resident appeared.

At the mention of the name Sherlock Holmes he handed the dog over to me at once with no questions asked, and Toby — an ugly, short-haired mongrel with a clumsy, waddling gait — accompanied me willingly into the coach.

It had just turned four o'clock when I passed the two constables guarding the gates of Pondicherry Lodge with my unusual friend. Holmes was standing on the doorstep of the house, smoking his pipe.

"Ah, you have him," he said excitedly. "Well done, Watson. We have had an immense display of energy since you left. Athelney Jones has arrested not only friend Thaddeus but also the gatekeeper, the housekeeper and the Indian servant, and taken all of them off to Norwood Police Station. I think he even suspected you and me at one stage of the proceedings!"

In Holmes' hand was his handkerchief, now blackened with liquid. "I have just dipped this in the creosote spilled from the broken bottle in

Sholto's room," he explained. "We know that Number One trod in this substance, and with Toby's help we can pick up the scent."

He took the dog's stout leash from me and led him down to the drive. "Here you are boy," he said, putting the handkerchief under the creature's nose. "Good old Toby. Good dog. Smell it, boy!" He then threw the handkerchief well away into the bushes, and led Toby round to the back of the house. There, by a large water-barrel, the dog suddenly stopped and broke into a succession of high yelps; then, with his nose on the ground and his little tail wagging furiously, he pattered off on the trail of the villains at a pace which strained his leash.

To the east the sky had been gradually whitening, and we could now see some distance in the cold, grey light.

Our course led us across the untended gardens of the sad, massive house, until we reached the walls of the grounds. Above us there were several stones missing from the top of the wall, and it was obvious that this was the place the intruders had left, if not also entered, Pondicherry Lodge.

I confess I had my doubts about our being able to pick up the scent on the roads of outer London, even though there had been no rain in the many hours since the murderers had made their escape. But my fears were soon appeased as Toby, rarely hesitating or swerving from his course, sniffed his way along leafy pavements and across grassy heaths towards the great city.

"Do not imagine, Watson," said Holmes as we made our way through Dulwich, "that I depend for my success in this case on the mere chance of one of these fellows having stepped in some spilled chemical. I now have knowledge which would enable me to trace them in many different ways. This, however, is the readiest, and since fortune has put it into our hands, I should be at fault to ignore it. Nevertheless, it has prevented this case from becoming the pretty intellectual problem that at one time it promised to be. There may have been some credit to be gained out of it but for this convenient clue."

"There is credit enough," I said. "I assure you, Holmes, that I marvel at the means by which you obtain your results. The thing seems to me to be deeper and even more inexplicable than before. How, for example, could you describe the wooden-legged man to Jones with such confidence?"

"It was simplicity itself, my dear Watson. Two officers in command of a penal settlement learn an important secret to buried treasure. A map is drawn for them by an Englishman named Jonathan Small; you remember we saw the name on Miss Morstan's chart. He had signed it on behalf of himself and his three associates — the sign of four, as he somewhat dramatically called it. Aided by this chart, one of the officers, Major Sholto, gets the treasure and brings it to England. Now then, why did Small not get the treasure himself? The answer is obvious. The chart is dated at a time when Morstan was brought into association with the convicts; Small did not get the treasure because he, and presumably his associates, were convicts and could not get away."

"But this is mere speculation," I remarked.

"It is more than that, Watson; it is the only explanation which covers the facts. Let us see how it fits in with later events. Major Sholto remains at peace for some years, content in the possession of the treasure. Then he receives a letter from India which gives him a great fright. What could that be about?"

"A letter to say the men whom he had wronged had been set free," I suggested.

"Or escaped," said Holmes. "That is far more likely, since he would have known what their term of imprisonment was. So what does he do then? He guards himself against a wooden-legged man — a white man, mark you, for he mistakes a tradesman for him and actually fires at him. Now, only one white man's name is on the chart: the others are Hindus or Muslims. Therefore we may say with some confidence that

the wooden-legged man is identical with Jonathan Small. Does the reasoning strike you as faulty?"

"No," I answered. "It's clear and concise."

We were by now setting out across some parkland, still following the unerring nose of the trusty Toby.

"Well now," continued Holmes, "let us put ourselves in the place of Small. He comes to England with the double idea of regaining his treasure and of having his revenge on the man who had wronged him. He finds out where Sholto lives, and very possibly sets up communications with someone in the household. He cannot find out, however, where the treasure is hidden, for no-one ever knew except the major and one faithful servant, who had died.

"Suddenly Small learns that the major is close to dying. In a frenzy, lest the secret of the treasure die with him, he runs the gauntlet of the guards, makes his way to the dying man's window, and is only deterred from entering by the presence of Sholto's two sons. He knows that they have seen him but, mad with hate, he enters the room later that night, searches the dead man's papers in some hope of discovering some clue to the whereabouts of the treasure, and finally leaves a memento of his visit by way of the inscription on a note. He had no doubt planned that, should he slay the major, he would leave some such record on the body, as a sign that it was not a common murder but, from the point of view of the four, something in the nature of an act of justice. Strange whims of this kind are not unusual in the annals of crime, and often provide valuable clues to the identity of the criminal. Do you follow all this?"

"Yes, very clearly."

"Good. But what can Small do now? He can only continue to keep a secret watch on the efforts made to find the treasure. It may be that he leaves England and only comes back at intervals. Then comes the discovery of the treasure, and he is immediately informed of it; again we trace the presence of some confederate in the household. Small, with his wooden leg, is unable to reach the lofty room of Bartholomew Sholto. He takes with him, however, a curious associate, who solves this problem for him but dips his foot into creosote. Hence Toby and a long walk for you and me, my dear doctor."

"But it was the associate who committed the murder, not Small."

"Quite so, Watson, and no doubt to the anger of Small. He bore no grudge against Bartholomew Sholto, only his father, and would probably have preferred simply to have the poor man bound and gagged. He did not wish to put his head in a noose, but there it is."

We had for the best part of our journey been following Toby down the villa-lined roads that led to the metropolis. Now, however, we were beginning to come among more crowded streets, where labourers and dockers were already about, and women were taking down shutters and washing down doorsteps.

Our quarry seemed to have taken a strangely zigzag route, for we had traversed Dulwich, Streatham, Brixton, Camberwell and Kennington, and we now found ourselves in Nine Elms, approaching a large timber-yard bordering the river. Here Toby suddenly darted down a track towards the water. We followed him onto a small jetty and here, with our guide waddling around in circles and whining, the trail came to an abrupt end.

7 The Baker Street Irregulars

Two or three small boats lay in the water by the jetty, and Toby was taken to each of them in turn. But he made no sign.

"We are out of luck," said Holmes. "It appears they have taken to a boat."

Close to the landing-stage was a house with a wooden placard hanging up outside it. '*Mordecai Smith*' was printed across it in large letters and, underneath, '*Boats to hire by the hour or day*'. A second inscription above the door told us that a steam launch was kept — a statement confirmed by a great pile of coal nearby.

"It is probably our men who have taken the steam launch," said Holmes. "Come, Watson, let us try to find out."

His loud knock on the door was answered by a dumpy, round-faced woman.

"Good morning, Mrs Smith," said Holmes, removing his hat. "I'm so sorry to disturb you so early. Is your husband at home, by any chance?"

"No, sir, he's been away since yesterday morning. To tell the truth, I'm beginning to get worried about him. But if it was about a boat, maybe I could serve as well?"

"I wanted to hire his steam launch."

"Why, it's the steam launch he's gone out in, sir. That's what puzzles me, for I know there's no more coals in her than would take her to Woolwich and back. If he'd been away in the barge I'd have thought nothing — many a time he's been right down to Gravesend in her, and stayed over."

"He may have bought coal further down the river," suggested Holmes.

"He might, sir, but it weren't his way, not at the prices they charge for a bag. Besides, I don't like that wooden-legged man and his big talk."

"Wooden-legged man?" said Holmes, trying hard to feign lack of interest.

"Yes, a monkey-faced chap who's called more than once to my old man. It was him that roused him up yesternight — three in the morning it was — and my man knew he was coming, too, for he had steam up in the launch. I tell you straight, gentlemen, I don't feel easy in my mind about it."

"My dear Mrs Smith, I'm sure you are getting worried about nothing," said Holmes casually. "Tell me, was the wooden-legged man alone?"

"Couldn't say, sir. I only saw him, and didn't hear nor see no-one else."

"I'm sorry, Mrs Smith. I wanted the steam launch, and I've heard good reports of the — let me see, what's her name?"

"The *Aurora*, sir."

"Ah! She's not that green one with a yellow line, very broad in the beam?"

exhaust them."

"Employ the police, then."

"No, I shall probably call in Jones at the last moment. He is not a bad fellow, and I should not like to injure him professionally, but I have a fancy to work it out myself now that we've gone so far."

"What are we to do, then?" I asked as we landed at Millbank.

"We will take a hansom cab, drive home, have some breakfast, and get an hour's sleep. It is quite on the cards that we may be afoot again tonight. We will keep Toby, for he may be of use to us yet."

On the way we pulled up at Great Peter Street Post Office, and Holmes dispatched a wire.

"Whom do you think that was to?" he asked as we resumed our journey.

"I'm sure I don't know," I replied.

"You remember the Baker Street division of the detective force that I employed in the Jefferson Hope case?"

"Well?" said I, laughing.

"This is just the case where they might be invaluable. That wire was to my dirty little lieutenant, Wiggins, and I expect he and his gang to be with us shortly after we have finished breakfast."

It was between eight and nine o'clock now, and I was starting to feel the effects after the long night. I was limp and weary, foggy in mind and fatigued in body. I did not have the professional enthusiasm that carried my companion on, nor could I look at the matter as a mere abstract

"No, sir, no! She's as trim a little thing as any on the river. She's been fresh painted, black with a red stripe."

"Thank you. I hope you will hear soon from Mr Smith. I am going down the river, and if I should see anything of the *Aurora* I shall let him know that you are concerned. A black funnel, you say?"

"Black with a broad white band, sir."

"Of course. Well, good morning, Mrs Smith."

We walked downstream a little and caught a rowing boat across the river.

"She was extremely helpful to us," I said as we crossed the now busy waters of the Thames.

"The main thing with people of that sort," replied Holmes, taking out his pipe, "is never to let them think that their information can be of the slightest importance or use to you. If they do they will instantly shut up like an oyster. If you listen to them under protest, as it were, you are very likely to get what you want."

"Our course of action now seems pretty clear," I said after a pause.

"Yes? What would you do, then, Watson?"

"I would engage a launch and go down the river on the track of the *Aurora*."

"My dear fellow, it would be a colossal task. She may have touched at any wharf on either bank between here and Greenwich. Below London Bridge there is a perfect labyrinth of hiding places for miles. It would take us days to

problem with no emotion or feeling. But a bath and complete change at Baker Street freshened me up wonderfully. When I came down to our room I found the breakfast ready and Holmes himself pouring out the coffee.

I had hardly begun my ham and eggs when there was a loud and long ring at the bell, and I could hear Mrs Hudson raising her voice in a wail of dismay.

"By heavens, Holmes!" I said, half rising. "I believe they've come after us!"

"It's not quite that bad," said Holmes, with a wide smile. "It's the unofficial force — the Baker Street Irregulars."

As he spoke, there came a swift pattering of feet on the stairs, a clatter of high voices, and at the door there appeared a group of dirty and ragged little street boys.

"Got yer message, sir!" said one, taller and older than the others.

Holmes walked slowly over towards them, wagging his finger. "In future they can report to you Wiggins, and you to me. I cannot have the house invaded in this way. Now, I want you to find the whereabouts of a steam launch called the *Aurora* — owner Mordecai Smith, black with two red stripes, funnel black with a white band. She is down the river somewhere. I want one boy to be near Smith's landing-stage opposite Millbank to say if the boat comes back. You must divide it out among yourselves and do both banks thoroughly. Let me know the moment you have news. Is all that clear?"

"Yes, guv'nor," replied Wiggins.

"The old scale of pay, plus a guinea to the boy who finds the boat. Here's a day in advance. Now off you go."

Holmes handed them a shilling each, and away they buzzed down the stairs.

"If the launch is above water they will find her," said Holmes after they had gone. "They can go everywhere, see everything, overhear everyone. I expect to hear before evening that they have spotted her. In the meantime, we can do little but await results. We cannot pick up the broken trail until we find either the *Aurora* or Mordecai Smith."

After breakfast I joined Holmes by the fire, and suddenly felt sleepy. "Are you going to retire to bed for a while?" I asked him.

"No, I'm not tired. I have a curious constitution. I cannot remember ever feeling tired by work, though idleness exhausts me completely. I am going to smoke and think over this queer business. If ever a man had an easy task, Watson, this one of ours ought to be. Wooden-legged men are hardly common, and the other man should, I think, be just about unique!"

"Yes, the other man again," I said.

"I have no wish to make a mystery of him to you, doctor. But you must have formed your own opinion by now. Consider the data: small footprints of naked feet, toes never fettered by shoes, great agility, poisoned darts. What do you make of all that?"

"Some sort of native," I suggested.

"Hmm, those little darts could only be shot in one way: from a blow-pipe. Now, then, where do we find our savage?"

"South America?" I offered.

Holmes did not answer, but took down a bulky book from the shelf.

"This is the first volume of a gazetteer which has just been published," he said. "Let us see: *'Andaman Islands, situated 340 miles to the north of Sumatra in the Bay of Bengal.'* What's all this? Humid climate, coral reefs, sharks, convict barracks, cottonwoods — ah, here we are: *'The aboriginal people of the Andaman Islands may perhaps claim the distinction of being the smallest race on this earth. The average height is rather below four feet, although many full-grown adults can be much smaller. They are a fierce, intractable people, but capable of forming the most devoted friendship once their confidence has been gained.'"*

"But how did he come to have such a weird companion?" I asked.

"That, Watson, is more than even I can tell. Since we have already determined that Small had come from the Andamans, however, it is not that surprising that an islander be with him. No doubt we shall learn about all this in time. But you look all in. You lie down there, on the sofa, and I shall put you to sleep."

He took up his violin and, as I stretched myself out, began to play some dreamy melodious air — his own, no doubt, for he had a remarkable gift for improvization. I have a vague recollection of his figure and the rise and fall of his bow; then I seemed to be floating peacefully away on a soft sea of sound until I found myself in dreamland, with the sweet face of Mary Morstan looking down upon me.

8   A Break in the Chain

It was late in the afternoon when I woke, strengthened and refreshed. Holmes was standing by the fire, smoking his pipe.

"Is there any news," I asked.

"Unfortunately, no. I confess I am surprised and disappointed. I expected something definite by now. But Wiggins has just been up to report, and he says that no trace can be found of the launch. It is a frustrating delay."

"Can I do anything? I asked. "I'm fresh now, and quite ready for another night's work."

"No, we can only wait. You can do what you will, but I must remain here in case any message should come in."

"Then I shall go over to Camberwell and call on Mrs Forrester. She asked me to, yesterday."

"On Mrs Forrester?" asked Holmes with the twinkle of a smile in his eyes.

"Well, on Miss Morstan too, of course. They were anxious to hear about anything that happens. I shall be back in two or three hours."

"If you are crossing the river you may as well return Toby, for I don't think we'll be needing him now."

I took the little mongrel and left him, together with half a sovereign, at the good naturalist's in Pinchin Lane. It was well into evening before I left Camberwell, and dark before I reached Baker Street. My companion's pipe and book lay on his chair, and there was no note.

"You're driving yourself too hard over this matter," I said over breakfast, "and I speak as a doctor as well as a friend. I heard you marching about in the night."

"I could not sleep," he answered. "This infernal problem is consuming me. It is too much to be baulked by so petty an obstacle, when all else has been overcome. I know the men, the launch, everything; yet we have no news. I have set other things in motion and used every means at my disposal. The whole river has been searched on either side, but still there is no news; nor has Mrs Smith heard of her husband. I shall be forced to conclude soon that they have scuttled the craft."

"Or that Mrs Smith has put us on the wrong track," I suggested.

"I think we can dismiss that, Watson. I had

enquiries made, and her description of the launch is correct."

"Could it have gone up river?" I asked.

"I have considered that possibility, of course, and there is a search-party working up as far as Richmond. If no news comes today I shall start off myself tomorrow and try and find the men rather than the boat. But surely — surely — we will hear something soon."

We did not, however. Not a word came to us from any source. There were articles in most of the newspapers on the Norwood tragedy, all rather hostile to the unfortunate Thaddeus Sholto, but no fresh details were to be found except the notice of an inquest the following day. I walked over to Camberwell to tell the ladies of our lack of success, and on my return I found Holmes dejected and somewhat morose. So, with little left to accomplish, I turned in for an early night.

When I woke the next morning there was no sign of Holmes. I assumed that, even with his iron constitution and restless spirit, he was now catching up on some lost sleep. However, Mrs Hudson told me otherwise.

"Mr Holmes went out very early," she explained. "He said he did not know how long he would be, and it was not possible to contact him."

"Were there any instructions?" I asked.

"Yes, sir. You are to remain here at all times, in case of messages or calls. Mr Holmes said you were to act on your own judgment if any important news did come."

Over breakfast I read in the *Standard* that Sholto and the housekeeper, Mrs Bernstone, had been released the previous evening for lack of evidence. This was indeed a relief — though the report also stated that the case was still under the personal direction of Superintendent Athelney Jones.

It was a long, long day. Every time a knock came to the door or a sharp step passed in the street, I imagined it was Holmes returning or some crucial message.

At about three o'clock the boredom was broken by a loud voice in the hall, and no less a

person than Athelney Jones was shown in to me. Very different he was from the brusque tutor of common sense who had taken over at Pondicherry Lodge. His bearing was meek now, even apologetic.

"Good day, Dr Watson. Good day," said he. "Mr Holmes is out, I understand."

"Yes, Superintendent, and I cannot be sure when he will be back. Perhaps you would care to wait. Would you like a drink?"

"Thank you, I don't mind if I do. I'll have a whisky and soda."

I poured him his drink and handed it to him.

"I have been obliged to reconsider my theory in the Norwood case," he said after sitting down and taking a sip. "I had my net drawn tightly round Sholto when he went pop, right through it. He was able to prove an alibi which could not be shaken. From the moment he left his brother's room he was never out of sight of someone or other, so it could not be him who climbed over roofs and through trapdoors. It's a very dark case — and I should be glad of a little assistance."

"We all need help sometimes," I said.

"Your friend Sherlock Holmes is a wonderful man, sir," said he in a husky, confidential tone. "He's a man who's not to be beat. I never saw a case yet he could not throw some light on. He's irregular in his methods and a little quick in jumping at theories, but, on the whole, I think he'd have made a very promising officer in the force. Anyway, I had this wire from him late this morning, by which I understand he has got some clue to this Sholto business."

He took a telegram out of his pocket and handed it to me. It was dated Stepney, just

before twelve: '*Go to Baker Street at once. If I have not returned, wait for me there. I am close on the track. Come with us tonight if you want to be in at the finish.*'

"This sounds good!" I said. "He has evidently picked up the scent again."

We had only just started our second drink when Mrs Hudson knocked and entered. "There's an old gentleman here to see you, Dr Watson. He insists that he speaks to you personally."

"Very well, Mrs Hudson. Please show him up."

The housekeeper beckoned the man up the stairs. We heard steps and a great heavy wheezing, as from a man who was sorely short of breath, but at last he made his way to our door and Mrs Hudson showed him in. He was an old, stooping, bearded man, clad in seafaring clothes. He had a coloured scarf round his neck and I could see little of his face except a pair of keen, dark eyes, overhung by bushy brows. Altogether he gave me the impression of a master mariner who had fallen on bad times.

"What is it, my man?" I asked.

He looked about him, slowly and methodically, before answering. "Is Mr Sherlock Holmes here?" he inquired in a breathy voice.

"No, but I am acting on his behalf. You can tell me any message you have for him."

"It was to him that I was to tell it," said he.

"But I am acting for him in all matters. Was it about Mordecai Smith's boat?"

"Yes. I knows where it is. And I knows where the men are that he's after. And I knows where the treasure is. I knows all about it."

"Then tell me," I said, with a touch of impatience, "and I shall tell him."

"It was to him that I was to tell it," he repeated obstinately.

"Well, if you insist, then you must wait for him."

The old man came across and sat down on the sofa, resting his face on his hands, and Jones and I resumed our talk.

Suddenly, however, Holmes' familiar voice broke in on us. "I think you might offer me a drink, too."

As we turned to him the old man peeled off his scarf, his eyebrows and his whiskers — and there sat my companion!

"Holmes!" I cried. Good heavens — it's you!"

"I thought my disguise was pretty good, gentlemen, but I hardly expected it to pass a test such as that."

"You rogue!" cried Jones, seemingly delighted. "You would have made an actor and a rare one. You had the proper workhouse cough, and those shaky legs of yours are worth ten pound a week. I thought I recognized the eyes, though."

"I have been working in this get-up all day," explained Holmes, accepting the drink I offered him. "You see, many of the criminal classes begin to know me — especially since my friend here took to publishing some of my cases. So I can only go on the warpath under some disguise like this."

"What made you choose these clothes?" I asked.

Holmes took several sips of his drink. "I worked on the problem most of the night. My boys had been up the river and down the river, both banks, with no result. The launch was nowhere, nor had it returned. Yet it was unlikely it had been scuttled, though that always remained a possibility. Now, Small must have felt that the strange appearance of his associate would attract attention, however they may have disguised him. It was three o'clock when they picked up the launch, according to Mrs Smith, so in order to hide the vessel in darkness they could not have gone far. People would soon be about. Therefore, I deduced, they paid Smith well to hold his tongue, reserved the launch for the final escape, and hurried to their lodgings with the treasure.

"In a couple of nights, when they had seen what the papers were saying, when they could see if there was any suspicion, when the pressure was off, they would return to the launch, and go downstream to some larger vessel where, no doubt, they had booked their passages to another continent."

"But what about the whereabouts of the launch?" I asked.

"I could think of only one thing; Small must have put it in the hands of some boat-builder or repairer, with orders to make some trifling change in her. She would then be removed from the water to his yard or shed, and be therefore concealed from view, while at the same time he

could have her made ready at a few hours' notice."

"That all seems simple enough," said the Superintendent.

"It is just these simple things which can so easily be overlooked," said Holmes. "This morning, in this seaman's rig, I began to inquire at all the yards down the river. I drew a blank at the first fifteen, but at the next — Jacobson's at Wapping — I learned that the *Aurora* had been handed over to them two days ago by a red-haired man with some small directions as to her rudder.

"'There ain't nothing amiss with her rudder,' said the foreman. 'There she lies, with the red stripes.' At that moment who should appear but Mordecai Smith, the owner, rather the worse for drink. 'I want the *Aurora* tonight at eight,' he

bellowed. 'Eight sharp, mind, for I have two gentlemen who won't be kept waiting.'

"I followed Smith some distance then, but he disappeared into an alehouse. I found a post office to wire you, Superintendent, then went back to the river and, chancing to see one of Wiggins' boys, still searching, posted him as sentry over the yard. He is to wave his handkerchief to us when they start out. We shall be lying off in the river, and it will be a strange thing if we do not take men, treasure and all."

"You have planned it all very neatly," said Jones, "but if the affair were in my hands I should have had a body of police in Jacobson's Yard, and arrested them when they came down."

"This man is a shrewd fellow, Superintendent. He may well send a scout on ahead — perhaps the red-haired man — and if anything made him suspicious he would lie snug or try some other route of escape."

"You could have stuck to Smith," I suggested, "and be led to their hiding-place — and the treasure, if it's not hidden on board."

"I think it is a hundred to one against Smith knowing where they live, Watson. As long as he had excellent pay and plenty of liquor, why should he ask awkward questions? They send him messages what to do, I'll wager. No, I have thought over every possible course of action, and this is the best."

Holmes stood up and put his glass down on the table. "You are welcome to all the official credit in this, Superintendent, but in return you must put yourself under my orders. Is that agreed?"

"Entirely," replied the detective, "if you help me to the men."

"Good. In the first place I shall need a fast police boat — a steam launch — to be at the Westminster Stairs at seven tonight."

Athelney Jones nodded.

"Then I shall want two good men in case of resistance."

"There will be two or three in the boat, as well as stokers. What else?"

"I should very much like to hear something of this matter from the lips of Small himself. You know I like to work the details of my cases out. Do you object to my having an unofficial interview with him, here in my rooms or elsewhere, provided he is efficiently guarded?"

"Rather an irregular proceeding," replied Jones, shaking his head. "But then this whole affair is irregular, and I suppose we must wink at it. If you can catch Jonathan Small, I don't see how I can refuse you an interview with him."

The detective made his way to the door, keen to get on with the arrangements. "Is there anything else, Mr Holmes?" he asked as he was about to leave.

"Only one thing, Superintendent: I suggest that for our own protection we all carry revolvers on our mission tonight."

Athelney Jones gestured agreement with his hand, then disappeared down the stairs.

9 The End of the Islander

The face of Big Ben showed just before seven when we arrived at the Westminster Stairs and found our launch awaiting us. Holmes eyed it critically.

"Is there anything to mark it out as a police boat from a distance?" he asked Jones.

"Yes, those green lamps on the sides."

"Then take them off, Superintendent."

This done, we stepped on board and the ropes were cast off. Jones and I stood in the bow, with Holmes behind us. There was one man at the wheel, an engineer-captain and two stokers.

"Where to?" asked Jones.

"To Rotherhithe. Tell them to stop across the river from Jacobson's Yard in Wapping."

Our craft was evidently a very fast one. We shot past the long lines of loaded barges as though they were stationary, and Holmes smiled with satisfaction as we overhauled a river steamer and left her far behind us.

The bridges seemed to fly over us, and soon we reached Tower Bridge, the last one. After that we slowed down and crept nearer to the south bank, close to the maze of boats and barges at Rotherhithe.

"That is Jacobson's Yard," said Holmes, pointing to a bristle of masts and rigging on the north side. "Cruise gently up and down here under cover of this long string of barges."

He took a pair of binoculars from his coat and gazed some time on the other shore. "I see my trusty sentry at his post," he said, "but no sign of a handkerchief. Still, they are hardly likely to be early."

"Suppose we go downstream a short way and lie in wait for them," suggested Jones eagerly.

"We cannot take anything for granted," replied Holmes firmly. "It is odds-on that they will go downstream, of course, but we cannot be certain. From this point we can see the entrance

of the yard, but they will find it difficult to see us. We must stay where we are."

The police boat cruised as quietly as it could up and down, patrolling behind the barges. Several times I checked my watch, and when it approached a quarter past eight I began to suspect that something had gone wrong.

"Over there, Watson!" shouted my companion suddenly. "Look, over there! Do I see a handkerchief? Surely it is a white flutter?"

"Yes, it is your boy," I replied. "I can see him plainly."

"And there is the *Aurora*!" exclaimed Holmes, "going like the devil! Full speed ahead, engineer! Make after that launch with the red stripe. By heaven, I shall never forgive myself if she proves to have the heels of us!"

Our quarry had slipped unseen through the yard entrance and passed between two or three large craft, so that she had got a good speed up before we saw her. Now she was flying down the river, close to the shore, going at a tremendous rate. Jones looked gravely at her and shook his head.

"She's very fast," he said. "I doubt if we shall catch her."

"We *must* catch her!" cried Holmes between his teeth. "Heap it on, stokers! If we burn the boat we must have them!"

We were fairly after her now. The furnaces roared, and the powerful engines whizzed and clanked like a great metallic heart. Her prow cut through the still water and sent two rolling waves to right and to left of us. With every throb of the engines we sprang and quivered like a living thing. One great yellow lantern in our bows threw a long, flickering funnel of light in front of us. Right ahead a dark blur on the water showed where the *Aurora* ran, and the swirl of white foam behind her spoke of the pace at which she was going. We flashed past barges, steamers, merchant vessels, in and out, behind this one and round the other. Voices hailed us

out of the darkness, but still the *Aurora* thundered on, and still we followed close on her track.

"Pile it on, men, pile it on!" cried Holmes, looking down into the engine-room, while the fierce glow from below beat upon his eager face. "Get every pound of steam you can."

"I think we're gaining a little," shouted Jones with his eyes on the *Aurora*.

"I'm sure of it," said I. "We shall be up with her in a very few minutes."

At that moment, however, as the evil fates would have it, a tug with three barges in tow blundered in between us. It was only by putting our helm hard down that we avoided a collision, and before we could round them and recover our way the *Aurora* had gained a good two hundred yards. She was still, however, well in view.

Our boilers were now strained to their utmost, and the frail shell vibrated and creaked with the fierce energy which was driving us along. We had shot through the Pool, past the West India Docks, down the long Limehouse Reach, and up again after rounding the Isle of Dogs. The dull blur in front of us resolved itself now clearly into the dainty *Aurora*. We could see now the figures on her deck. One man stood at the wheel, with something black between his feet. In the bow lay a bundle, covered with a coat or blanket.

Between them I could see Smith, stripped to the waist, and shovelling coals for dear life. They may have had some doubt at first as to whether we were pursuing them but now, as we followed every winding and turning which they took, there could no longer be any question about it. At Greenwich we were about three hundred paces behind them; at Blackwall we could not have been more than two hundred and fifty. I have coursed many creatures in many countries during my checkered career, but never did sport give me such a wild thrill as this mad, flying manhunt down the Thames.

Steadily we drew in on them, yard by yard. In the silence of the night we could hear the panting and clanking of their machinery. At one point the man in the stern crouched down on the deck, and his arms were moving as though he were busy with something. Nearer we came, and nearer, then Jones yelled at them to stop. We were not more that four lengths behind them now, both boats flying at a tremendous pace. It was a clear reach of the river, with Barking Level on one side and the desolate Plumstead Marshes on the other. At our hail the man at the wheel turned and shook his clenched fist at us, cursing

all the while in a high, cracked voice. He was a short but powerful man, and as he stood poising himself with legs astride I could see that from the thigh downwards there was but a wooden stump on the left side.

At the sound of his strident, angry cries, there was movement in the huddled bundle on board. It straightened itself into a little black man — the smallest I have ever seen — with a great, misshapen head and a thick, red headband. Holmes had already drawn his revolver, and I whipped out mine at the sight of this savage, distorted creature. He was wrapped in some sort of blanket, which left only his face exposed, but that face was enough to give a man sleepless nights. Never have I seen features so deeply marked with malice. His small eyes glowed and burned, and his thick lips were writhed back from his teeth, which grinned and chattered at us with half animal fury.

"Fire if he raises his hand to his mouth," said Holmes firmly.

We were within a boat's-length by this time, and almost within touch of our quarry. I can see

the two of them now as they stood, the white man shrieking out curses, and the dwarf with his hideous face, his strong yellow teeth gnashing at us in the light of our lantern.

It was well that we had so clear a view of him. Even as we looked he plucked out a short, round piece of wood, and put it to his lips. Our pistols rang out together. He whirled round, threw up his arms, and, with a choking cry, fell headlong into the swirling water.

The next moment the wooden-legged man threw himself on the wheel and put it hard down, so that his boat made straight for the southern bank, while we shot past her stern, only clearing her by a few feet. We were round after her in an instant, but she was already nearly at the bank. It was a wild and desolate place, where the moon glimmered on a wide expanse of marshland, with pools of stagnant water and beds of decaying vegetation.

With a dull thud, the launch ran up on the mud-bank, her bow in the air and her stern flush with the water. First Smith and then the fugitive sprang out, but his stump instantly sank its whole length into the sodden soil. He struggled

and writhed, but not one step could he take forward or backward. He yelled in impotent rage and kicked frantically into the mud with his other foot, but his struggles only bored his wooden pin deeper into the sticky bank. When

we brought our launch alongside he was so firmly anchored that it was only by throwing the end of a rope over his shoulders that we were able to haul him out and to drag him, like some evil fish, over our side.

"See here, Watson," said Holmes, pointing to the wooden hatchway. "We were hardly quick enough with our pistols." There, sure enough, just behind where we had been standing, stuck one of those murderous darts which we knew so well. It must have whizzed between us at the instant we fired. Holmes smiled at it and shrugged his shoulders in his easy fashion, but I confess that it turned me sick to think of the horrible death which had passed so close to us that night.

10 The Strange Story of Jonathan Small

A solid iron chest stood on the deck of the *Aurora*, and this was now transferred to the police launch. Then, as we began to move back upstream — the boat's searchlight looking in vain for the lost islander — we gathered round the cause of this whole tangled affair.

"Where's the key, Small?" demanded Jones.

"I haven't got it," sneered the prisoner. "I threw it into the river."

"Did you now? Well, we'll just have to break it open then, won't we?"

A constable was ordered to fetch a crowbar from below and, after some difficulty, he prised the heavy lid open. Then we all gaped in utter astonishment and disbelief: the chest was completely empty! There was not a trace of a single gem!

Small grinned triumphantly, but he refused to tell Jones where the treasure was, despite all kinds of threats. The detective was furious at being cheated, but after some persuasion he agreed to Holmes' suggestion to resume the discussion in the comfort of Baker Street.

In our room at 221B, Small sat stolidly in his chair. He was not yet fifty, and his face was not an unpleasant one, though his heavy brows and aggressive chin gave him, as I had witnessed, a terrible expression when moved to anger.

I poured everyone a large drink, including the prisoner, for I felt this was going to be a long evening.

"Right, Small!" began Jones, towering over his man. "What have you done with that treasure?"

"I've put it away where you can never lay hands on it," he cried exultantly. "It's my treasure, and if I can't have the loot I'll take darned good care that no-one else does. No living man has any right to it, unless it is three men who are in the Andaman barracks. I know now that I can't have the use of it, and I know that they can't. I've acted all through for them as much as for myself. It's always been the sign of four with us, and I know that they would have had me do just what I have done, and throw the treasure into the Thames rather than let it go to kith or kin of Sholto or Morstan. You'll find the treasure where the key is and where little Tonga is — at the bottom of the river."

"You're deceiving us, Small," said Jones. "If you'd wished to throw the treasure into the Thames, it would have been easier for you to have thrown the lot — chest and all."

"Easier for me to throw — and easier for you to recover," he answered with a shrewd, sideways look. "The man that was clever enough to hunt me down is clever enough to pick an iron box from the bottom of a river. Now that they are scattered over five miles or so, it will be a harder job."

"This is a very serious matter, Small," said the detective. "If you had helped justice, instead of obstructing it in this way, you would have had a better chance at your trial."

"Justice!" snarled the prisoner. "A pretty justice! Whose loot is this, if it is not ours? Where is the justice that I should give it up to those who have never earned it? Look how I've earned it! Twenty long years in that fever-ridden swamp, all day at work under the mangrove-tree, all night chained up in the filthy convict-huts, bitten by mosquitoes, racked with pain. That was how I earned the Agra treasure. I would rather swing a score of times, or have one of Tonga's darts in my hide, than live in a convict's cells and feel that another man is at his ease in a palace with the money that should be mine."

All this came out in a wild whirl of words, while his eyes blazed and the handcuffs clanked together with the impassioned movement of his hands. I could understand, as I saw the fury and the passion of the man, that it was no groundless or unnatural terror which had possessed Major Sholto when he first learned that the injured convict was on his track.

"You forget that we know nothing of all this," said Holmes quietly. "We have not heard your story, and we cannot tell how far justice may originally have been on your side."

"Well, sir, you at least have been fair-spoken to me, though I can see that I have you to thank that I'm in chains. Still, I bear no grudge for that. It's all fair and above-board. If you want to hear my story, I have no wish to hold it back. What I say to you is God's truth, every word of it."

Small took up his glass with both hands and took several gulps of his drink.

"When I was eighteen I joined the army," he began, "and I was soon posted to India. I hadn't been out there long when I was fool enough to go swimming in a secluded river, and a crocodile took my left leg, just below the knee, as clean as a surgeon would have done it. After five miserable months in hospital I was discharged from the army as a cripple, and not yet twenty years old.

"After some time I managed to get a job as an overseer on a plantation. This meant a lot of riding on horseback — which, despite my leg, I found I could do well. Then, after some years, with no warning, the great mutiny was on us; my house was burned down and most of my friends and their families were slaughtered. I managed to reach the safety of Agra, where other British people had gathered under the protection of what remained of the garrison. There we lived for many months, in a virtual state of siege.

"One of my tasks was to guard, with two Punjabis, an isolated gate on the north-west side of the old fort, well away from the city and the main body of troops. On the third night of this duty these two Punjabis, Mahomet Singh and Abdullah Khan by name, suddenly threatened me at knifepoint. Khan told me that I must be either with them or against them in their plan to become rich; they needed my help — but would kill me there and then if I refused.

"He knew of a wealthy rajah in the north of the country who had joined the mutineers. This prince had kept all his gold and silver at his palace, but had sent all his most precious jewels to Agra with a trusted servant. If the rebels won, he would say he was on their side and keep his gold and silver: if the British won, his jewels would be safe in Agra.

"Mahomet Singh then told me that this servant, Ahmed by name, was already inside the city of Agra but needed to gain access to the safety of the fort. He had as his travelling companion Singh's half-brother, Dost Akbar, who knew the secret. Dost Akbar had arranged to lead him to a gate in the wall that night — the gate I was guarding. There we would kill him, and the great treasure of the rajah would be split four ways.

"I agreed to their plan, and we exchanged solemn oaths of loyalty, equality and secrecy. I shall spare you the gruesome details; let us say the deed was done and we buried the body of Ahmed in an isolated part of the old fort."

At this point he held out his glass for another drink, which I poured for him. I must confess that by now I felt that whatever punishment was in store for him, he could expect no sympathy from me — and I could see the same silent disgust in the faces of my companions. He must have sensed it, too, for here he suddenly went away from the narration.

"It was very bad, no doubt. But I should like to know how many men in my shoes would have refused a share of this loot when they knew the alternative was certain and swift death."

"Go on with your story," said Holmes firmly.

"We counted the jewels and I quickly made a list — and a very impressive list it was. We renewed our oath, then buried the treasure in a wall in the fort. The next day I drew up four identical plans of the place, and put the sign of four at the bottom of each one. We had sworn that each of us would always act for all, and this is an oath that I can put my hand to my heart and swear that I have never broken.

"The mutiny was put down a few months later, and we were just beginning to think we

105

could retrieve our shares of the plunder when all four of us were arrested for the murder of Ahmed. I could hardly believe it. The suspicious rajah had, it seemed, put another servant to follow Ahmed to Agra, and this second servant decided, when the mutiny was over, to inform the British of what he suspected. The body was eventually found, but no mention was ever made of the treasure, for the second servant knew nothing of its value. All of us were sentenced to penal servitude for life, and sent to the Andaman Islands."

"It should have been death," interrupted Jones. "That's what you deserved for cold-blooded murder!"

"I was the only white prisoner on the Andamans," continued Small, "and with good behaviour I soon enjoyed something of a trusted and privileged position, including assistant to the doctor. I discovered after some time that Major Sholto and, to a lesser degree, Captain Morstan, were in considerable bad debts from playing cards with the civilians who worked at the settlement. Well, to make a long story very

short, I did a deal with the two of them, for a fifth share of the treasure. The other three prisoners all agreed to my scheme.

"I was to provide both Sholto and Morstan with charts of the Agra fort, showing where the treasure was hidden. Sholto was to go to India to test our story. If he found the treasure, he was to leave it there, send out a small yacht with provisions for a long voyage for after our escape, and return to his duties. Morstan was then to apply for leave of absence and meet us at Agra. There we were to divide the treasure, with Morstan taking care of Sholto's share as well as his own until they could meet in England.

"Well, the villain Sholto went off to India and never came back. Morstan followed as soon as he could, and found the treasure gone. From that time I lived for only one thing: vengeance. My only thought, day and night, was to escape, track down Sholto, and have my hand on his throat.

"But it was many years before my chance came. It started one day when a little islander was picked up by a convict-gang in the woods.

106

He was sick to death and had gone to a lonely place to die. I took him in hand and nursed him, and in two months he was well again. He took a fancy to me and was always hanging around my hut, so I befriended him.

"His name was Tonga, and he owned a big canoe. When I found that he was devoted to me and would do anything to serve me, I saw my chance. On the night of the planned escape, however, there happened to be one of the convict-guards down at the wharf — a vile Pathan who had never missed an opportunity to insult or injure me. I could see no weapon, so I unstrapped my wooden leg and knocked his skull in with it. You can still see the split in the wood where I hit him. Anyway, we made our escape, and were eventually picked up by a Malay ship heading for Singapore."

We were all struck dumb by this amazing account, not least by the casual way in which the prisoner recalled his second killing.

"Well," resumed Small, fully aware of the impact of his story, "if I were to tell you all the adventures that my Tonga and I went through I would have you up until the sun was shining. We drifted here and there about the world, something always turning up to keep us from London. All the time, however, I never lost sight of my purpose. I would dream of Sholto at night. A hundred times I have killed him in my sleep. At last, however, some three or four years ago, we found ourselves in England. I had no great difficulty in finding where Sholto lived, and I set to work to discover whether he still had the treasure. I made friends with someone who could help me — I name no names, for I don't want to get anyone else in a hole — and I soon found that he still had the jewels. Then I tried to get at him in many ways; but he was pretty sly and always had two prize-fighters, besides his sons and servants, to guard over him.

"One day, however, I got word that he was dying. I hurried at once to the garden, and that he should slip out of my clutches and, looking through the window, I saw him with his sons. I'd have come through and taken my chance with the three of them, only even as I looked at him his jaw dropped, and I knew that he was gone. I got into his room that same night, though, and searched his papers to see if there was any record of where he had hidden our jewels. But there was nothing, so I came away.

"Before I left I scrawled down the sign of four,

as it had been on the chart, and I pinned it on his chest. It was too much that he should be taken to the grave without some token from the men whom he had cheated.

"We earned a living at this time by my exhibiting poor Tonga at fairs and other such places as the black cannibal. He would eat raw meat and dance his war-dance, so we always had a hatful of pennies after a day's work. I still heard all the news from Pondicherry Lodge, but for some years there was none to hear, except that they were still hunting for the treasure. At last, however, came what we had waited for so long. The treasure had been found. It was up at the top of the house in Mr Bartholomew Sholto's laboratory. I came at once and had a look at the place, but I could not see how, with my wooden leg, I was to make my way up to it. I learned, however, about a trapdoor in the roof, and also about Mr Sholto's supper-hour. It seemed to me that I could manage the thing easily through Tonga. I brought him out with me with a long rope wound round his waist. He could climb like a cat, and he soon made his way through the roof. But, as ill-luck would have it, Bartholomew Sholto was still in the room.

"Tonga thought he had done something very clever in killing him, for when I came up by the rope I found him strutting about as proud as a peacock. He was very much surprised when I made at him with the rope's end and cursed him. I took the treasure-box and let it down, and then slid down myself, having first left the sign of four on the body to show that the jewels had at last

come back to those who had most right to them. Tonga then pulled up the rope, closed the window, and made off the way that he had come."

"Well, Jonathan Small," said Holmes, "I am sorry it has come to this."

"And so am I, sir," replied the prisoner. "But I don't believe that I can swing for the job. I give you my word that I never raised a hand against Mr Sholto. It was that little hell-hound who shot one of his poisoned darts into his neck. I had no part in it. The truth is that I expected to find the room clear. I knew the habits of the house pretty well, and it was the time that Mr Sholto usually went down to his supper. If it had been the old major I would swing for him with a light heart, but it's hard that I should be lagged over this young Sholto, with whom I had no quarrel."

"I think I can prove that the poison acts so quickly that the victim was dead before you ever reached the room," said Holmes.

"That he was, sir. Thank you. I don't know that I have much else to tell you. I had heard a waterman once speak of the speed of Smith's launch, so I engaged her for our escape. He was to get a handsome sum if he got us safe to our ship — the *Esmeralda*, at Gravesend, bound for Brazil. He knew nothing of our secrets. He was simply paid well to keep quiet and get us to our ship."

"A very remarkable account," said Holmes. "A fitting end to an extremely interesting case. There is nothing at all new to me in the latter part of your narrative except that you brought your own rope. That I did not know."

"Well, Holmes," said Jones, "you are a man to be humoured, and we all know that you are a connoisseur of crime. But duty is duty, and I've gone rather far in what you asked me. I shall feel more at ease when we have our little story-teller here safely under lock and key. I'm much obliged to both of you gentlemen for your assistance. You will be wanted at the trial, of course. Goodnight to you."

The huge detective and the little prisoner made their way to the door.

"You first, Small," said Jones as they left the room. "I'll take care that you don't club me with your leg, whatever you may have done to that poor fellow in the Andamans."

"Well, there is the end of our drama," I remarked as I stood at the window, watching Jones bundle Small into the back of the police wagon. But tell me, Holmes, who was the spy at Pondicherry Lodge?"

"They had, as I surmised, a confederate in the house, who could be none other than Lal Rao, the butler. So Jones actually had the undivided honour of having caught one guilty fish in his great haul!"

"The division seems rather unfair," I said. "You have done all the thinking and hard work in this business. Jones gets the credit, I fall in love; but what remains for you?"

"The work itself, the satisfaction of solving the mystery — that is prize enough for me, my dear doctor. And now goodnight, Watson; I suddenly feel very weary."

"Goodnight, Holmes," I replied. "And pleasant dreams."

The Hound of the Baskervilles

Introduction

IN 1901 the many Sherlock Holmes fans were delighted to see the appearance of a new adventure featuring their hero — *The Hound of the Baskervilles*, published in nine monthly instalments in *The Strand Magazine*. Arthur Conan Doyle had actually "killed off" Holmes in 1893 when, in *The Final Problem*, the famous detective and his arch-rival Professor Moriarty, locked in a deadly clinch, plunged into the swirling waters below the Reichenbach Falls in Switzerland. *The Hound of the Baskervilles* was set well before that, but by October 1903, with *The Empty House*, we find Holmes' "death" explained away and his creator (by now knighted by King Edward VII) was, by popular demand, to continue writing stories about him until 1927.

The Hound of the Baskervilles is by far the best known of all the Sherlock Holmes stories — a wonderful combination of family ghosts, sinister moors and a frightening creature of the night. It was inspired by Doyle's journalist friend Fletcher Robinson, who during a wet golfing holiday in Norfolk in March 1901 entertained Doyle with tales of his native Devon. One of these was about a legend of a ghostly giant hound, and the writer's imagination was at once fired by it — so much so that the following month the two men spent several days exploring the moors around Princetown, home of the notorious Dartmoor Prison.

It seems that at first it did not occur to Doyle to use Holmes in the story, but when he realized that he needed such a central character he decided to fall back on his established hero rather than go to all the trouble of inventing another one. Thus a whole era of new Sherlock Holmes adventures was born.

More than most of the other Holmes stories, *The Hound of the Baskervilles* is full of fascinating characters, as well as the "regulars". There is the man who takes the case to Baker Street, Dr Mortimer, at times resembling a mad scientist rather than a quiet country doctor; there is the naturalist Stapleton, flitting about the deserted moors with his butterfly net; there is the shadowy figure of the bearded butler, Barrymore, the eccentric but charming Mr Frankland, and the haunting presence of Selden, the violent Notting Hill murderer.

To begin with it is Holmes' trusted aide Dr Watson who follows up the bizarre clues and tries to unravel the mystery — and by the time Holmes makes his dramatic reappearance, events have indeed moved far and fast.

1   The Curse of the Baskervilles

Sherlock Homes had many intriguing requests for help, but none as strange as that asked by Dr James Mortimer, from Devon, who called on us at 221B Baker Street one bright morning in the autumn of 1890.

Since it was Mrs Hudson's day off, Holmes himself answered the front door and showed our visitor up the stairs to our room. Mortimer was a tall, gaunt man, with a long chin and a beak-like nose that supported a pair of gold-rimmed spectacles, and his jacket seemed almost to be falling off as he crossed the room towards me.

"May I present Dr John Watson," said Holmes by way of introduction. "A professional brother to you, and a vital assistant to me."

"I'm glad to meet you, sir," he replied. "I've heard your name mentioned in connection with that of your friend."

He declined my suggestion of coffee and took the seat offered to him.

"I come to you, Mr Holmes," he began, "because your fame as an unraveller of mysteries has spread even to the backwaters of Devon, and I have a problem that only a man of your intellect can resolve."

"What is the precise nature of this problem?" asked Holmes.

Dr Mortimer took from his bag an old manuscript and handed it to my companion. I peered over his shoulder at the heading: *'Baskerville Hall'* it said, and below, in large scrawling figures, *'1742'*.

"It appears to be a statement of some kind," said Holmes.

"Yes, it's a statement of a legend which runs in the Baskerville family, written in old English. It is, I'm sure, connected with the matter on which I wish to consult you and, with your permission, I will condense it for you."

"Please do," said Holmes, returning the paper to Mortimer and taking out his pipe and tobacco.

"Thank you. The legend states that some generations ago one Sir Hugo Baskerville, a wild and cruel man hated by the local people, became besotted by the daughter of one of his yeomen, and one drunken night he abducted her and locked her in a bedroom at Baskerville Hall. While Sir Hugo and his friends celebrated the success of taking this maid against her father's wishes, the terrified girl escaped through a small window and fled into the night. When Sir Hugo discovered this he dragged his grooms from their beds to saddle his horse and fetch his hounds, and then took off to hunt the girl down.

"He whipped up his horse and sped like the wind across the Devon moors. Some of his friends eventually followed, and soon they passed three night shepherds on the moorlands. The story goes that these men were so crazed with fear they could hardly speak, but one did tell them that they had seen the maiden, and Sir Hugo on his black mare — but also, and here I read, Mr Holmes, 'behind him such a hound of hell as God forbid should be on any man's heels'.

"Eventually these friends found Sir Hugo's dogs, whimpering at the top of a hill, from where they could see, by the light of the moon, right down into a small valley. What they witnessed sickened and terrified them. The maid lay fallen, dead from fear and fatigue; nearby was Sir Hugo's body, and standing over it was, and again I quote, 'a great black beast shaped like a giant hound yet larger than any hound any man

has ever seen, which was at that very moment, with blazing eyes and flashing fangs, ripping mouthfuls of flesh from the dead man's throat'.

"These petrified witnesses returned to Baskerville Hall, there to relate their dreadful tale. And the son of Sir Hugo later wrote it all down — as a warning to the Baskervilles of what lies in wait for them on dark nights on the moor."

Dr Mortimer pushed his spectacles down his great nose a little way and handed the manuscript back to my companion.

"Well, Mr Holmes, do you find it interesting?"

"As a fairy tale, yes," he replied.

"In that case I will give you something a little more recent and factual," said Mortimer. "About three months ago a very good friend of mine, Sir Charles Baskerville, died in suspicious circumstances late at night near Baskerville Hall."

"Yes, I read the coroner's report in the newspapers," interrupted Holmes. "If I remember correctly he concluded that Sir Charles died of natural causes — a heart attack, in fact."

"That is so," resumed Mortimer. "But there is far more to it than that. That fateful evening I had myself dined with Sir Charles at the Hall and, against my advice, he insisted on going for his usual late-night stroll. We went some way together, then we parted company and I walked home. But he never returned. After some time Barrymore, the butler, went looking for him, and found his body some distance from the house. He then sent Perkins, the young groom, to come and fetch me. There were no signs of violence on Sir Charles' person, but there was the most incredible distortion of the face; this, as I well know, is not uncommon in cases of death from heart attack. Those are the public facts in the case."

"And what of the private ones," inquired Holmes.

"In giving you those," replied Mortimer, now showing some signs of emotion about the whole matter, "I'm telling you that which I have told no-one. I withheld it from the coroner's inquest because a man of science shrinks from appearing to endorse a popular superstition. I had the further thought that the Hall would probably remain untenanted and therefore fall into decay if anything were to increase its already rather grim reputation. For both these reasons I told less than I knew, but with you I can and will be perfectly frank."

"Please go on, Dr Mortimer," said Holmes.

"Over the last few months of his life it became increasingly plain to me that Sir Charles' system was strained to near breaking point. He was convinced that some dreadful fate hung over the family, and the image of some ghastly presence haunted him constantly. As his doctor I was well aware of his weak heart, and I suggested he go to London for special treatment; indeed he was due to go the very next morning. Mr Stapleton, a mutual friend, was of the same opinion.

"On the night of his death I carefully inspected the body. Sir Charles lay prostrate, his arms out, his fingers dug deep into the earth, and his features convulsed as I have described.

Now, one false statement was made by Barrymore at the inquest when he said there were no traces of anything in the ground near the body. He did not see any; but I did — some distance away on the path, but fresh and clear."

"Footprints?" suggested Holmes.

"Footprints," replied Mortimer.

"A man's or a woman's?"

Dr Mortimer looked strangely at us for a moment, then his voice sank almost to a whisper as he gave his answer: "Mr Holmes, they were the footprints of a gigantic hound!"

I confess that a shudder passed through me at these words, but Holmes leaned excitedly forward and shot a barrage of questions at the poor doctor — about the path, the gate, the hedge, even about the weather — all of which our visitor answered clearly and concisely.

At last Holmes slapped his knee and stood up. "Dr Mortimer, if only you had called me in earlier, when the matter was fresh."

"I could not call you in then without disclosing these facts at the inquest. Besides, well —"

"Yes, why do you hesitate?"

"There is a realm in which even the best of detectives is helpless."

"You mean that the thing is supernatural," suggested Holmes. "Not of this world."

"Mr Holmes, I find that before this terrible event occurred several people had seen a creature on the moor which corresponds with this Baskerville demon, and which could not possibly be any animal known to science. They all said it was a huge creature, luminous and ghostly. I assure you that there is now a reign of terror in the district, and hardly any man will cross the moor at night."

"And you, a trained man of science, believe it to be supernatural?"

"I don't know what to believe, Mr Holmes. That's why I have come to you. I only want to find out the truth."

My companion shrugged his shoulders. "I have so far confined my investigations to this world," said he. "I have in a modest way combatted evil, but to take on the devil himself would, I think, be too ambitious a task. Yet you must admit that the footprints were real."

"The original hound was real enough to tear a man's throat out, according to the legend," replied Mortimer.

Holmes lit his pipe and walked slowly round the room. "In what way do you think I can assist you?"

"By advising me as to what I should do with Sir Henry Baskerville, who arrives at Waterloo Station this very afternoon."

"Is he the heir to the estate?" I asked.

"Yes, Dr Watson, he is Sir Charles' nephew and the next of kin. On the death of Sir Charles we found that he had been farming and travelling in North America for some years, and is an excellent chap, by all accounts."

"There is no other claimant, I suppose?" asked Holmes.

"None. The only other kinsman whom we could trace was Roger Baskerville, the youngest

of the three brothers; Sir Charles was the eldest. The middle son was the father of Henry, but Roger was the black sheep of the family. He was the image of Hugo, they tell me, and behaved even worse. He fled the country to Central America, and died there of yellow fever in 1876. So, Sir Henry is the last of the Baskervilles. I have had a wire that he arrived at Southampton this morning. Now, Mr Holmes, what do you recommend me to do with him, as executor of his uncle's will?"

"I recommend, sir, that you take a cab and proceed to Waterloo Station to meet Sir Henry Baskerville, as planned."

"And then?"

"And then you will say nothing to him about all this until I have made up my mind about the matter."

"How long will that take?" asked Mortimer.

"Less than twenty-four hours. I would be very much obliged if you will call on me here at ten o'clock tomorrow, bringing Sir Henry with you."

"I will do so, Mr Holmes," replied our visitor with some relief. "Good day, gentlemen, and thank you."

2   Sir Henry Baskerville

Our clients were punctual, for the clock had just struck ten when Dr Mortimer was shown in to our rooms, followed by the young baronet. He was a sturdily-built man of about thirty, with a strong face dominated by a thick, reddish moustache. He had the weather-beaten appearance of one who has spent most of his time in the open air, yet there was something in his steady eye and his bearing which indicated the gentleman.

"This is Sir Henry Baskerville," said Dr Mortimer.

"I'm pleased to meet you two gentlemen," he said in a distinctly North American accent. "The strange thing is, Mr Holmes, that if Dr Mortimer here hadn't suggested coming round to see you I might still have come of my own accord. I understand you solve little mysteries; well, I received one this morning in the form of this letter."

He handed the envelope to Holmes, who studied it carefully. "Hmm. '*Sir Henry Baskerville, Northumberland Hotel, London W.1.*', printed in rough characters. The postmark is Charing Cross, early last evening. Who knew that you were going to stay at the Northumberland, Sir Henry?"

"That's just it — no-one could have known. We only decided after I met Dr Mortimer, and he's been staying with friends."

"Someone appears to be taking a deep interest in your movements," said Holmes, taking out the contents and spreading it on the table. Across the single sheet of paper a sentence had been formed by pasting down printed words. It ran: '*If you value your life or your reason, stay away from the moor.*' Only the word 'moor' was printed in ink, and then far bigger than the rest.

"What do you make of that, Dr Mortimer?" asked Holmes. "You must admit there is

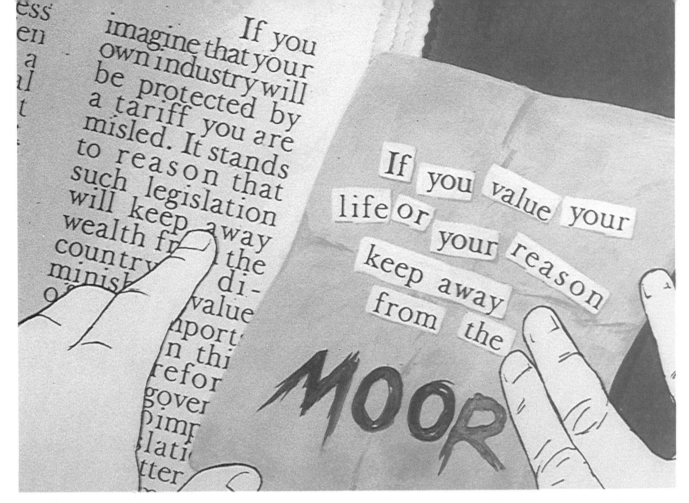

nothing supernatural about this, at any rate."

"No, sir, but it might well come from someone who was convinced that the business is supernatural."

"What business?" asked Sir Henry, sharply. "It seems to me that all you gentlemen know a great deal more than I do about my own affairs."

"You shall share our knowledge before you leave this room, Sir Henry," said Holmes. "I promise you that. For the present we will confine ourselves, with your permission, to this very interesting document. Might I trouble you for yesterday's *Times*, Watson — the page with the leading articles?"

I fetched the newspaper from the rack and handed it to him at the page requested. He gave me the note, then ran his eyes up and down the columns of the paper.

"Yes, here we are, gentlemen, the article on free trade. Permit me to read you an extract from it: '*You may imagine that your own special trade or your own industry will be aided by a tariff, but it stands to reason that such laws must in the long run keep away wealth from the country and lower the general conditions of life in this land.*'"

Dr Mortimer looked at Holmes with an air of professional interest, but Sir Henry turned a pair of puzzled eyes on me. "It probably makes good sense," he said, "but aren't we getting off the track of the letter just a little?"

"On the contrary, Sir Henry, we are hot upon it. Watson here knows my methods."

"I confess I see no connection," I said.

"And yet, my dear Watson, there is a very close connection indeed. Hand me the note."

Holmes put the note on the table, with the newspaper alongside it, and ran his finger along the article. "If — you — value — your — life — or — your — reason — keep away — from — the — and the word 'moor' is written by hand. Whoever composed the letter could not find the word 'moor' in the newspaper. Any doubts are settled by the fact that the words 'keep away' are cut out in one piece."

"You know you're right!" cried Sir Henry. "That's incredible. How did you do it?"

"The type style of a *Times* leading article is quite distinctive," explained my companion, "and the words can have been taken from nothing else. As the letter was put together yesterday — and almost certainly late yesterday — it was probable that the words were taken from yesterday's edition."

"Really, Mr Holmes, this exceeds anything I

could have imagined," said Dr Mortimer. "What else can you deduce from the message?"

"Notice that the address on the envelope and the word 'moor' are written in rough characters, yet the *Times* is read by well-educated people. We can take it, therefore, that the letter was composed by an educated man who wishes to disguise his writing — for fear that it may be recognized by you, Sir Henry, at some time in the future. The other point is that we can take it he is not ill disposed towards you, since he warns you of impending danger."

"It seems to me, gentlemen," said Sir Henry, with a touch of frustration, "that it's time you kept your promise and gave me a full account of what this is all about."

"Your request is a very reasonable one," replied Holmes. "Dr Mortimer, I think you could not do better than to tell your story as you told it to us."

Our scientific friend drew the manuscript from his case and presented the whole scheme as he had to us the previous morning. Sir Henry listened intently, with the occasional exclamation of surprise.

"Well, I seem to have come into an inheritance with a vengeance," he said when Mortimer had finished. "Of course, I've heard of the hound ever since I was in the nursery — it's the great story in the family. But I'd never thought of taking it seriously before."

"The practical point we must now decide, Sir Henry," said Holmes rather sternly, "is whether or not it is advisable for you to go to Baskerville Hall."

"Why shouldn't I go?"

"There seems to be danger."

"Do you mean danger from this fiend — or danger from other humans?"

"That is what we must find out."

"Whichever it is, Mr Holmes, my answer is the same. There is no devil in hell, and there's no man on earth, who can stop me going to the home of my own people, and you may take that to be my final answer."

His brows knitted and his face flushed to a dusky red as he spoke. "Meanwhile, I've hardly had time to think all this over. I'd like to have a quiet hour to myself. It's half-past eleven now, and I'm going straight back to my hotel.

Suppose you and your friend, Dr Watson, come around and lunch with us at one o'clock. I'll be able to tell you more clearly then how this thing strikes me."

"Is that convenient to you, Watson?"

"Perfectly," I replied.

"Then you may expect us, Sir Henry. Shall I have a cab called?"'

"I'd prefer to walk, thank you. This affair has flustered me a little."

"I'll join you in the walk if I may," said Mortimer.

"Then we meet again at one," said Holmes. "Good morning, gentlemen."

As soon as we heard the front door close behind our visitors Holmes changed from the languid dreamer to the man of action.

"Your coat and boots, Watson! Quick! Not a moment to lose!"

We hurried down the stairs and out into the street; Sir Henry and Dr Mortimer were just still in sight.

"Shall I run on and stop them," I asked.

"Not for the world, my dear Watson. I am perfectly satisfied with your company, if you will tolerate mine. No, it is quite evident that Baskerville has been closely shadowed since his arrival in London — or else how could it have been known so soon that he was at the Northumberland. And if he was followed the first day, he will probably be followed on the second."

He quickened his pace until we were no more than a hundred yards behind our friends. Then, still keeping our distance, we followed them into Oxford Street and down Regent Street. Once they stopped to look in a shop window, and we did the same. A moment later Holmes gave a little shout of satisfaction, and I followed the gaze of his eager eyes to a hansom cab on the other side of the street. It had halted, but was now walking on again.

"There's our man, Watson! Come on! We'll have a good look at him, if we can do no more."

And little more could we do, for no sooner was

I aware of a bearded face turned on us from the cab when the figure yelled something to the driver, and the cab flew off down Regent Street. We looked round for another to follow, but none was in sight.

"Confound it!" cried Holmes. "What bad luck — and bad management, too. We have not only lost our man, but betrayed ourselves in the process."

"What a pity we didn't get the number," I said.

"My dear Watson! Clumsy as I may have been, you surely don't imagine that I would let the cab go without noting its number? In fact, 2704 is our man. But that's of little use at the moment. Could you swear to the man's face?"

"I could swear only to the beard," I replied. "And that could be false."

"Indeed, Watson, you could well be right. It appears we are dealing with a clever fellow in this matter. Come, let us have a glass of wine before we go on to the Northumberland."

We arrived at the hotel a few minutes early, and with good reason. Holmes, in his unique fashion, discovered from the clerk the names, occupations and appearance of the few persons who had registered there as guests after Sir Henry — and none could possibly be our quarry. He then requested the clerk to send a boy round to the official registry of London cabs, trace the owner of 2704, and have him

come to Sir Henry's room as soon as possible.

At one o'clock exactly, we were greeted in Sir Henry's suite by the baronet and Dr Mortimer.

"Did you know that you were followed to Baker Street and then back here again this morning?" asked Holmes.

"Followed?" asked Mortimer. "By whom?"

"That we cannot say, unfortunately. He slipped away. But tell me, doctor, have you among your neighbours or acquaintances on Dartmoor any man with a full, black beard?"

"Let me see. Why, yes — Barrymore, Sir Charles' butler. He has a black beard. But he's in Devon now, in charge of the Hall."

"We had best check if he is really there. Hand me a telegram form, Watson. *'Is all ready for Sir Henry?'* That will do. Address to Mr Barrymore, Baskerville Hall. Which is the nearest telegraph office? Combe Tracey. Right, we will send a second wire to the postmaster, Combe Tracey: *'Telegram to Mr Barrymore to be delivered into his own hand. If absent, please return wire to Sir Henry Baskerville, Northumberland Hotel, London.'* That should let us know by tonight whether Barrymore is at his post in Devonshire — or not."

"Tell me, Mortimer," asked Sir Henry, "what can you tell me about this Barrymore?"

"He's the son of the old caretaker, who has long been dead. The family have looked after the Hall for generations. So far as I know, he and his wife are as respectable as any couple in the county."

"Did Barrymore profit at all by Sir Charles' will?" asked Holmes.

"He and his wife received five hundred pounds each."

"And did they know they would receive this?"

"Yes, Mr Holmes. But I hope you are not looking with suspicion on everyone who received a legacy from Sir Charles, since I had a thousand pounds left to me."

"Indeed! Anyone else, doctor?"

"There were many small sums to individuals and a large number of public charities. The rest all went to Sir Henry."

"And how much was that, may I ask?"

"It was seven hundred and forty thousand pounds in all."

Holmes raised his eyebrows in surprise. "I had no idea that so large a sum was involved," he said. "It is a stake for which a man might well play a desperate game. And one more question, Dr Mortimer: supposing that anything happened to our friend here — you will forgive the unpleasant thought — but who would inherit the estate?"

"Since Roger Baskerville, Sir Charles' younger brother, died unmarried and childless, the estate would descend to the Desmonds, who are distant cousins. James Desmond is an elderly vicar in Westmorland, and he once came down to Devon. He is a saintly man, and I remember that he refused to accept any settlement from Sir Charles."

"Thank you, the details are always of great interest to me. But I think that is all for the present."

We retired to lunch, and I asked Sir Henry if he had decided on his course of action.

"I sure have," he replied. "I'm going down to Devon in the morning."

"On the whole I think your decision is a wise one," said Holmes, "but you must not go alone."

"Dr Mortimer returns with me."

"But Dr Mortimer will have his practice to run and his house is several miles from yours, I understand. With all the will in the world, he may be unable to help you. No, Sir Henry, you must take with you a trusty man who will always be at your side."

"Could you come yourself, Mr Holmes?"

"If matters came to a crisis I should try to be present in person. But you can understand that,

with my consulting practice and the constant appeals that reach me from many quarters, it is not possible for me to leave London."

"Whom would you recommend, then?"

Holmes looked unerringly in my direction. "If my friend here would undertake it there is no man who is worth more at your side when you are in a tight spot. And no-one can say that more confidently than I."

The suggestion and the compliment took me completely by surprise, but before I had time to answer Baskerville was already thanking me.

"I will come with pleasure," I said. "I could not employ my time better."

"I'd planned to take the 10.30 train from Paddington, Dr Watson. Would that suit you, too?"

"Perfectly," I replied, already a little excited at the prospect of adventure.

"Good," said Holmes, rubbing his hands. "Then that is all settled."

We were enjoying our coffee after lunch when there was a loud knock at Sir Henry's door. The caller was a short, squat man — and the owner of cab number 2704. He came in and stood before us, hat in hand.

"I got a message that a gent at this address had been enquiring for 2704," he said. "I've driven my cab these seven years and never so much as a whisper of complaint. So I came here straight from the yard to ask you what you might have against me."

"I have nothing in the world against you, my good man," replied Holmes. "On the contrary, I have half a sovereign for you if you will give me clear answers to my questions."

"Well, I've had a good day and no mistake," said the cabbie, grinning. "What was it you wanted to know, sir?"

"Tell me about the fare who took you to watch my house in Baker Street this morning, and afterwards followed these two gentlemen here down into Regent Street."

The man looked surprised and a little embarrassed. "Why, there's not much good my telling you things, sir, since you seem to know as much as I do already. The truth is that the gent told me he was a detective — and that I was to say nothing about him to anyone."

"Did he say anything more?"

"He mentioned his name, sir."

Holmes cast a swift glance of triumph at me. "Oh he did, did he? How unwise. And what was this name he mentioned?"

"His name," said the cabbie carefully, "was Mr Sherlock Holmes."

Never have I seen my friend more completely

taken aback than by that cabbie's reply. For an instant he stood in silent amazement, then burst into a hearty laugh. "A touch, Watson — an undeniable score!" he cried. "I feel a foil as quick and supple as my own. So his name was Sherlock Holmes, was it? Excellent! Tell me where you picked him up, and all that happened."

"He hailed me in Trafalgar Square at about nine o'clock. He said he was a detective, and he offered me two guineas if I would do exactly what he wanted all day and ask no questions. First we drove down to the Northumberland Hotel, and waited there until two gentlemen came out and took a cab from the rank. We followed it until it pulled up in Baker Street and waited there an hour and a half. Then the two gents passed us, and we followed at a walk until well down Regent Street. Then he yelled that I should drive as fast as possible to Waterloo Station. He paid up his two guineas like a good 'un, and away he went. Just as he was leaving he turned round and said: 'It might interest you to know that you have been driving Mr Sherlock Holmes' — that's how I came to know his name."

"And how would you describe this Sherlock Holmes?" asked the real detective.

The cabbie scratched his head. "Well, I'd put him at about forty. He was middle height, two or three inches shorter than you, sir. Dressed like a toff, and a black beard, cut square at the end. I don't know that I could say more than that, sir."

"Well, here is your half sovereign. Thank you, and good day."

The cabbie departed, chuckling at his double luck, and Holmes turned to me with a rueful smile. "The cunning rascal. He knew that Sir Henry had consulted me, spotted who I was in Regent Street, guessed that I would have noted the number of the cab and would lay my hands on the driver — and so sent back this witty message. I tell you, Watson, this time we have a foe worthy of our steel. I've been check-mated in London, and I can only wish you better luck in Devon. It's an ugly business, Watson, an ugly, dangerous business, and the more I see of it the less I like it. I shall not sleep easy until I have you back safe and sound in Baker Street once more."

3   Baskerville Hall

The next day Holmes drove with me to Paddington Station, and as we waited on the platform he gave me his parting instructions and advice.

"I will not bias your mind by suggesting theories or suspicions," said he. "I wish you simply to report the facts in the fullest possible manner to me. The postal service is excellent."

"What sort of facts?" I asked.

"Anything which may seem to have a bearing on the case, however indirect, and especially the relations between young Baskerville and his neighbours; or of course any fresh particulars concerning the death of Sir Charles. I made some inquiries myself yesterday afternoon, but the only certain thing appears to be that Mr James Desmond, the heir, is an elderly gentleman of a very pleasant disposition, so I really think that we may eliminate him from our calculations. There remains the people who may actually surround Sir Henry Baskerville on the moor."

"Would it not be well in the first place to eliminate this Barrymore couple?"

"By no means, Watson. Indeed, you could not make a greater mistake. If they are innocent it would be a cruel injustice, and if they are guilty we would be giving up all chance of bringing it home to them. No, no, we will preserve them on our list of suspects. Then there is a groom at the Hall, if I remember right. There are two moorland farmers. There is this naturalist, Stapleton, and there is his sister — an attractive lady according to Dr Mortimer. There is Mr Frankland, of Lafter Hall, who is also an unknown factor, and there are one or two other neighbours. These are the folk who must be your special study. You are armed, I suppose?"

"I thought it as well to take my revolver."

"Certainly, Watson, and keep it near you night and day."

Our friends had already secured a compartment and now approached us on the platform.

"Good morning," said Dr Mortimer. "You

will wish to hear, Mr Holmes, that last evening Sir Henry received a reply from Barrymore — at Baskerville Hall."

"Well," said Holmes pensively, "that would seem to indicate that your butler is not the man following you around London, at least."

"We've not been followed since you frightened him off," added Dr Mortimer. "We've kept a sharp watch, whether together or alone, and no-one could have escaped our notice."

"I beg you not to go out alone in Devon, Sir Henry," said Holmes sternly. "Some great misfortune may befall you if you do."

The train began to glide down the platform. "Bear in mind, Sir Henry," continued Holmes, "one of the phrases of that queer old legend that Dr Mortimer has read to us, and avoid the moor during the hours of darkness. Goodbye — and good luck!"

The journey to the West Country was a pleasant one, and I spent most of it in getting to know better my two fellow passengers. Despite the strange cloud that hung over him, Sir Henry was excited and eager to arrive, for he had never been to Devon before, and as we caught our first glimpse of the moor I could sense both pride and determination in his face. The thought struck me then that if a dangerous quest lay before me, here was a comrade who would bravely share it with me.

The train pulled up at a small wayside station, and beyond the white fence a carriage was waiting for us. It was a peaceful country spot, but by the gate there were two soldierly men in dark uniforms, with rifles slung over their shoulders.

"What's all this, Perkins?" asked Mortimer of the groom.

"There's a convict escaped from the prison at Princetown, sir. He's been out three days now, and the warders watch every station, but they've had no sight of him. The folks about here don't like it, sir, and that's a fact."

"Well, I understand that they can get five pounds if they can give information."

"Yes, sir, but the chance of five pounds is but a poor thing compared to the chance of having your throat cut. It isn't like any ordinary convict you see, sir. This is a man who would stick at nothing."

"Who is he?" I asked the groom.

"It is Selden, sir, the Notting Hill murderer."

I remembered the case well, for it was one in which Holmes had taken an interest on account of the ferocity of the crime and the brutality which had marked all the actions of the assassin. But the death sentence had been changed to life imprisonment because of doubts about the sanity of the guilty man.

With this rather chilling news we boarded the carriage and headed away from the station. At every turning Baskerville gave an exclamation of delight, looking eagerly about him and asking countless questions. To his eyes all seemed beautiful, but to me a tinge of melancholy lay upon the countryside, which bore so clearly the marks of the waning year. The rattle of our wheels died away as we drove through drifts of rotting leaves — sad gifts, it seemed to me, for nature to throw before the returning heir.

Soon we topped a small hill, and in front of us loomed the huge expanse of the moor, mottled with gnarled rocks and craggy tors. A cold wind swept down from it and set us shivering. Somewhere out there, on that desolate plain, was lurking this fiendish man, hiding like a wild beast, his heart full of hate against the whole race who had cast him out. It needed only this to complete the grim picture of the barren waste, the chilling wind, and the darkening sky. Even Baskerville fell silent and pulled his coat more closely round him.

A few minutes later we approached Baskerville Hall, a forbidding building of granite, and as our carriage pulled up outside it a tall, bearded, balding man came down the steps towards us.

"Good afternoon, Sir Henry," he said, bowing slightly. "Welcome to your ancestral home. My name is Barrymore."

Dr Mortimer completed the introductions and then, after declining an offer of dinner from the new master of the Hall, went off in Sir Henry's carriage to his home.

Inside, it was very much as I had expected an old baronial home to look, but Sir Henry looked around in boyish amazement as Barrymore took us on a tour of its vast rooms. Later, he approached us both in the library.

"Would you wish dinner to be served at once, Sir Henry?" he asked.

"Is it ready?"

"In a very few minutes, sir. You will find hot water in your rooms. My wife and I will be happy, Sir Henry, to stay with you until you have made fresh arrangements, but you will understand that under these new conditions this house will require a considerable staff."

"Only when it is quite convenient to you, Sir Henry."

"But your family have been with us for generations. I will be sorry to begin my life here by breaking an old family connection."

There were signs of emotion on the butler's face. "I also feel that, sir, and so does my wife. But to tell the truth, we were both very much attached to Sir Charles, and his death has made these surroundings very painful to us. I fear that we shall never again be easy in our minds at Baskerville Hall."

"But what do you intend to do?"

"I have no doubt, sir, that we shall succeed in establishing ourselves in some business or other. Sir Charles' generosity has given us the means to do so. And now, sir, perhaps I had best get back to my duties."

We dined in the dark gloomy dining-room and, after a tiring day, retired early to our adjoining rooms. I wrote a short note to Holmes telling him of the day — and especially of the convict — before getting into bed. Yet I could not sleep well. Then quite suddenly, in the dead of night, there came a strange sound to my ears: it was the sound of a woman's sob, the muffled gasps of someone torn by uncontrollable sorrow. Then it died away, and as it did so there was the creak of footsteps past my room. There was no sound after that except the chiming of the clock and the rustle of ivy on the walls outside, and eventually I fell asleep.

"What new conditions, Barrymore?"

"I only meant, sir, that Sir Charles led a very retired life, and we were able to look after all his needs. Naturally you will wish to have more company, and so will require changes in your household."

"Are you trying to say that your wife and you wish to leave?"

4 The Stapletons of Merripit House

The fresh beauty of the following morning did much to erase the grim impression we had both gained on our first evening at Baskerville Hall.

"I guess it is ourselves and not the house we have to blame," said Sir Henry over breakfast. "We were tired with our journey and chilled by our drive, so we took a grave view of the place."

"And yet it was not entirely a question of imagination," I answered. "Did you, for example, happen to hear someone sobbing in the night — a woman I think — or any footsteps outside our rooms?"

"That's funny. When I was half asleep I did think I heard something. I waited quite a time, but there was no more of it, so I reckoned it was all a dream. But I heard no footsteps."

"I heard it all distinctly," I replied, "and I'm sure it was the sob of a woman."

He rang the bell and asked Barrymore about the incident. The butler looked uncomfortable as the baronet put his question.

"There are only two women in the house, Sir Henry. One is the scullery-maid, who sleeps in the other wing. The other is my wife, and I can say that the sound cannot have come from her."

It chanced then that Mrs Barrymore came in to take away the breakfast trolley, and as she did so she dropped some cups on the floor. As I looked around I could see from her swollen face and general manner that she had indeed been crying and was obviously still upset. Barrymore apologized for his wife's clumsiness and ushered her out, but it was quite apparent that the man had been lying.

Why had he, and why had she wept so bitterly? Already around this black-bearded man there was gathering an atmosphere of

"Surely his own wife ought to know where he was," said the postmaster a little testily. "Didn't he get the telegram? If there is any mistake it is for Mr Barrymore himself to complain."

It seemed hopeless to pursue the matter any further, but it was clear that in spite of Holmes' plan we had no real proof that Barrymore had not been in London all the time. As I walked back along the grey, lonely road, I prayed that my friend might soon be freed from his duties in the capital and come down to take this heavy burden of responsibility from my shoulders.

My thoughts were suddenly broken by a voice calling my name behind me. I turned, expecting to see Dr Mortimer, but to my surprise, it was a stranger who was pursuing me. He was a small, slim, clean-shaven, prim-faced man, between thirty and forty years of age, dressed in a grey suit and wearing a straw hat. A basket for collecting specimens hung over his shoulder, and he carried a green butterfly net in his hand.

"You will, I'm sure, excuse my presumption, Dr Watson," said he, as he came panting up to where I was. "Here on the moor we are homely folk and don't wait for formal introductions. You may possibly have heard my name from our mutual friend, Mortimer. I am Stapleton, of Merripit House."

"Your net and box told me as much," I replied, "for I knew that Mr Stapleton was a naturalist. But how did you know me?"

"I was calling on Mortimer, and he pointed

gloom and mystery. It was he who had been the first to discover the body of Sir Charles, and we had only his word for all the circumstances which led up to the old man's death. Was it possible that it was Barrymore, after all, whom we had seen in the cab in Regent Street? The first thing for me to do was to see the postmaster at Combe Tracey and find out whether the test telegram had really been placed in the butler's own hand.

Sir Henry had numerous papers to examine after breakfast, so it was a good opportunity for me to visit the village — a pleasant walk of three miles or so across the edge of the moor.

The postmaster had a clear recollection of the telegram.

"Certainly, sir," said he. "I delivered it to Mr Barrymore at the Hall, as directed, after I had finished here."

"Did you deliver it into his own hand?" I asked.

"Well, he was up in the loft at the time, so I couldn't do that, but I gave it to Mrs Barrymore, and she promised to take it to him at once."

"Did you see Mr Barrymore?"

"No, sir. I told you, he was in the loft."

"If you didn't see him, how could you know he was there?"

you out to me from the window of his surgery as you passed. Since my path led the same way, I thought I would overtake you and introduce myself. I also thought that you and Mr Holmes may have some new angle on our little mystery."

The words took my breath away for a second, but a glance at the placid face of my companion showed that no surprise was intended.

"It's useless for us to pretend that we don't know of you, Dr Watson," he said. "When Mortimer told me your name he could hardly deny your identity. If you are here, then it follows that Mr Holmes is interesting himself in the matter, and naturally I'm curious to know what view he might take of it all."

"I'm afraid I cannot answer that question," I said.

"May I ask if he is going to honour us with a visit himself?"

"He cannot leave town at present. He is engaged on other cases."

"What a pity! He might throw some light on those areas which are so dark to us. But as to your own researches, if there is any possible way in which I can be of service to you, I trust that you will ask me. If I knew a little more about your intentions I might even now be able to give you some help or advice."

"I assure you that I am simply here on a visit to my friend Sir Henry, and I need no help of any kind!"

"Excellent! You are perfectly right to be wary and discreet. I am justly rebuked for my intrusion, and I promise you I will not mention the matter again."

We walked on for some time together, and I accepted his invitation to Merripit House for some refreshment. As we strode further into the wastes of the moor he told me of his hobby and explained that though he had been there for less than two years, no-one knew the moor better. Then, with no warning, a dreadful cry echoed across the wasteland.

"Good heavens!" I cried. "What on earth is that?"

"It's probably one of the moor ponies," explained Stapleton calmly. "The mire has got her, I expect. You see that large dark green patch over there — that's the great Grimpen Mire. Even in the dry weather it's dangerous to cross it, but after the autumn rains it's a dreadful place. One false step means certain death to man and beast alike. Yet I can find my way to the very heart of it and return safely."

As he spoke a long, low moan drifted across the moor, swelling into a deep roar, then sinking back once more into a dull murmur.

"That's no pony!" I said.

"No, Dr Watson. Some of the local people say it's the Hound of the Baskervilles calling for its prey — for the blood of the lord of Baskerville Hall. I've heard it once or twice before, but never quite so loud. Do you know about the legend of the fiend-dog which is supposed to haunt the family?"

"I've heard of it, yes."

"It's extraordinary how stupid the peasants are about here," he said. "Any number of them are ready to swear that they have seen such a creature on the moor at night. Good lord, excuse me a moment, Dr Watson — that really is a beauty!"

He suddenly lurched off towards the mire, running in a zig-zag fashion after an elusive yellow butterfly, waving his net about frantically. As I watched him almost disappear into the green rushes, I was aware of someone behind me, and I turned to find a woman standing near me on the path. She had come from a direction in which a plume of smoke showed the position of Merripit House, but the dip of the moor had hidden her until she was quite close.

There was no doubt that this was the Miss Stapleton of whom I had been told, since ladies

I could only stare at her in silent surprise as her eyes blazed at me. "Why should I go back?" I asked.

"I can't explain," she said in a low, eager voice. "But for God's sake do what I ask. Go back, and never set foot on the moor again."

"But I've only just come."

"Can't you tell when a warning is for your own good? Go back to London, man! Start tonight! Get away from this place at all costs!"

At this she looked over my shoulder and put her finger to her lips. "Hush, my brother is coming. Please — not a word of what I have said."

Stapleton had abandoned the chase and now came back to us, breathing hard.

"What a pity I should have missed him," he panted. "You have introduced yourselves, I see."

"Yes," said his sister. "I was telling Sir Henry that it was rather late in the year for him to see the real beauty of the moor."

"What, Beryl! Who do you imagine this is?"

"I imagine that it is Sir Henry Baskerville, of course."

"No, no," said I. "Only a humble commoner, I'm afraid, though his friend. My name is Dr John Watson."

Her face flushed with embarrassment. "Oh, I see. I am sorry, Dr Watson. It seems we have been talking at cross-purposes."

of any kind must be few on the moor and she had been described as a beauty. The woman who approached me was certainly that, and with her perfect figure and elegant dress she was indeed a strange sight in that lonely place. Her eyes were on her brother as I turned, and then she quickened her pace towards me. I raised my hat and was about to introduce myself when she held up her hand.

"Go back!" she said. "Go straight back to London."

"Why, you didn't have much time for talk," her brother remarked with questioning eyes.

"I meant that I talked as if Dr Watson were a resident instead of a visitor," she said.

Stapleton affirmed his offer and we made the short walk to Merripit House, a bleak isolated farmhouse on the rim of the moor. As we waited for coffee I could not but wonder at what could have brought this educated man and this beautiful woman to live in such a place.

"Quiet spot to choose, isn't it?" he said, as though in answer to my thoughts. "But we manage to make ourselves fairly happy, don't we, Beryl?"

"Quite happy," said she, with no conviction in her voice.

"I had a school in the North," said Stapleton. "I enjoyed the life, but the fates were against us. A serious epidemic broke out there and three boys died. The school never recovered its reputation, and I lost a good deal of money. But I find an unlimited field of work here, and my sister is as devoted to nature as I am."

He talked at length about his interests in botany and zoology, but I was soon anxious to return to my charge. The melancholy mood of the moor, the death of the pony, the weird sound associated with the grim legend — all these things tinged my thoughts with sadness. Then there was the distinct warning of Miss Stapleton, delivered with such feeling that I could not doubt some grave reason lay behind it. I resisted all pressure to stay for lunch and, with my basic mission accomplished at Merripit House, set off on my return journey.

When I returned to Baskerville Hall I told Sir Henry at once how the matter of the telegram stood; and he, in his customary downright fashion, had Barrymore in there and then to ask him whether he had received the telegram. The butler said that he had.

"Did the postmaster deliver it into your own hand?" continued Sir Henry.

"No, sir. I was in the box-room at the time, and my wife brought it up to me."

"Did you answer it yourself?"

"No. I told my wife what to answer, and she went down to write it."

The words were the same as those Sir Henry had received, and, for the moment, the matter was considered closed.

That evening, however, Barrymore returned to the subject of his own accord, saying that he couldn't understand the reason for Sir Henry's questions and that he trusted that he had done nothing to forfeit the baronet's confidence. My friend had some job to pacify him, in fact, and finished by giving him a considerable part of his old wardrobe brought from Canada.

As a result of the strange sobbing and the footsteps, and then Barrymore's prickly attitude over the telegrams, Sir Henry and I decided to stay awake that night and try to solve the mystery. So, after writing my detailed report to Holmes in the library, we began our vigil.

Though we stayed up until past three o'clock in the morning, no unusual sound did we hear. Tired but undaunted, we nevertheless determined to try again the next night.

5 A Mysterious Light

The weather was unexpectedly bright and warm the next morning, and Sir Henry said that after his day of dull paperwork he was keen to go for a walk. I insisted I go with him, as instructed by Holmes, but after becoming somewhat agitated he persuaded me that my worries were unfounded.

Afterwards, however, I realized how wrong I had been; and so, rather than have words with him, I followed out of sight at a discreet distance. To act as the spy was a hateful task, but I feared for him even in broad daylight.

He had not gone far when he was met by none other than Beryl Stapleton. They had talked for some minutes when I spotted the unmistakable figure of her brother hurrying towards them. There then followed a strange scene in which Stapleton appeared to be abusing Sir Henry, while the sister looked on in silence. Finally he turned on his heel for Merripit House, dragging his sister forcibly with him.

I walked slowly up behind Sir Henry as he watched them go. He wheeled round on me and for a moment his eyes blazed, but my honest explanation soon satisfied him, and at last he broke into a rueful laugh.

"Did you see any of that, Watson? I think he must be crazy. I know there's a mad murderer loose out here, but do I look like him? He's acting more like a jealous husband than a protective brother. Mind you, she's certainly good looking — and there's a lot in her eyes that speaks louder than words."

As we continued our walk together Sir Henry explained that she had warned him to return to London and was convinced that his life was in danger. But she refused to say more. Indeed we were still puzzling over this when Stapleton arrived at the Hall that afternoon and, in the most dignified and charming manner, apologized for his rude behaviour to Sir Henry that morning. He explained that his sister meant everything to him, and that they had always been together. He was extremely sorry for his actions, and said he felt foolish and selfish. He concluded his little speech by inviting Sir Henry and myself to dine with him at Merripit House two evenings hence, and we accepted.

That night my companion and I tried our luck a second time to solve our domestic mystery — and got a good deal more than we bargained for. We had almost given up when, just before three o'clock, we heard the creaking of the boards outside our rooms. Moving out cautiously, we just saw the flickering light from a candle disappearing upstairs at the end of the corridor. We followed on tip-toe, and through the almost closed door of a large room we could make out the figure of a man at the window, passing the candle slowly to and fro across the glass.

I looked to Sir Henry for the next step, but before I could say or do anything he charged in and took the man, pinning him to the floor. The dropped candle went out, and as I grabbed the culprit's head Sir Henry re-lit it and pushed it close to his face. It was the bearded butler.

"All right, Barrymore, what in God's name are you doing up here?"

"Nothing, sir. It was the window. I always go round at night to see that they're all fastened."

"On the second floor?"

"Yes, sir — all the windows."

"Look here, Barrymore, we'll have the truth out of you, so it will save a lot of trouble for you to tell it sooner rather than later. Come on, man — no lies! Why were you holding a candle to the window?"

"Don't ask me, Sir Henry — don't ask me! I give you my word — it's not my secret, and I can't tell it. If it concerned only me I wouldn't keep it from you."

I took the candle from Sir Henry. "It must have been a signal," I said. "Let me try."

I held it as he had done, and after several seconds a pinpoint of light answered me from the darkness outside.

"There it is!" I cried. "A light out yonder."

"Now listen, you rogue," said the furious baronet. "Tell us who your confederate is out there on the moor — or you leave my employment this very night!"

"Then I must go, sir."

"And you go in disgrace. By thunder, Barrymore, you may well be ashamed of yourself. Your family and mine have shared this house for over a hundred years, and now I find you deep in some dark plot against me!"

"No, no, sir, not against you!" It was a woman's voice, and Mrs Barrymore, even more horror-struck than her husband, stood by the door. "It's all my doing, Sir Henry — all mine. John has done nothing except for my sake, and then only because I pleaded with him."

"Speak out, then. What does it all mean?"

"My poor brother is hiding out on the moor, sir. The candle is a signal to him that food is ready, and the light out yonder is to show us the place to take it."

"Then your brother is —"

"Yes, sir — Selden, the escaped convict."

Sir Henry and I both stared at the woman in amazement. It hardly seemed possible that this respectable person was of the same blood as one of the most notorious criminals in the country.

"Is this true, Barrymore?" asked Sir Henry.

"Yes, sir. Every word of it."

"Well, I can't blame your wife for trying to help her brother, or blame you for standing by your wife. Go to your room, and we shall talk further about this in the morning."

When they were gone we again looked out of the window. Sir Henry had flung it open, and the cold night air wind beat in on our faces. Far away in the distance there still shone that one tiny dot of yellow light.

"How far do you reckon that is, Watson?"

"Not more than a mile, I'd say, but it's difficult to tell."

"Well, it can't be that far if Barrymore had to carry out the food to it. He's waiting, this villain, beside that light. By thunder, Watson, I'm going to take him!"

driving across the face of the sky.

"I say, Watson," said Sir Henry as we left the Hall far behind, "what would Holmes say to this? What about that hour of darkness in which the power of evil is exalted?"

As if in answer to his words there rose out of the vast gloom of the moor that strange cry which I had already heard on the borders of the Grimpen Mire. It came with the wind through the silence of the night — a long, deep mutter, then a rising howl, and finally a sad moan in which it died away. Again it sounded, and again. The whole air throbbed with it — strident, wild, menacing. The baronet stopped in his tracks and looked at me.

"Good grief! What in God's name is that?"

"I don't know exactly. It's a sound of the moor. I heard it yesterday, when I was with Stapleton."

It died away, and silence closed in on us. We stood straining our ears, but nothing came.

"It was the cry of a hound," said Sir Henry.

There was a break in his voice which told of the sudden terror that had seized him.

"Tell me, Watson, what do the local people say of it? Come on, now, I'm not a child. You can speak the truth."

I hesitated but could not escape the question.

"They say it's the cry of the Hound of the Baskervilles."

The same thought had crossed my mind. It was not as if the Barrymores had taken us into their confidence; their secret had been forced from them, after all. The man was a danger to the community, a cruel murderer for whom there was neither pity nor excuse. We were simply doing our duty in grasping this rare chance of putting him back where he could do no harm.

"And I'll come with you!" I said.

The night air was heavy with the smell of damp and decay. Now and again the moon peeped out for a moment, but clouds were

He was strangely silent for a few moments. "A hound it was," he said, "and it seemed to come from miles away, over yonder. Isn't that the direction of the Grimpen Mire?"

"Yes, it is."

"Well, it was up there all right. My God, can there be some truth in all these weird stories, after all? Could I really be in danger from so dark a cause. That sound seemed to freeze my very blood!"

"Shall we turn back, Sir Henry?"

"No, by thunder, we won't. We've come to get our man, and we'll do it, Watson. Come on!"

We stumbled on in the darkness, the yellow speck of light burning steadily in front. Sometimes it seemed miles away, sometimes it seemed only yards from us. But at last we found the source of it, and it was strange to see this single lamp burning there in the middle of the moor, with no sign of life near it.

Then we both saw him. Over the rocks there was thrust out an evil, bristling face, scored with vile passions. Something had aroused his suspicions, and it may have been that Barrymore had a private signal which we had not given.

We knew that at any moment he may vanish into the night, and without speaking both Sir Henry and I dashed forward at the same moment. The convict screamed a curse at us

from above us and hurled a rock; then he shook his fist and I caught one glimpse of his strongly-built shape before he turned and ran, just as the moon broke through the clouds. We rushed to the top of the hill, and there was our quarry running down the other side, springing over the stones like a frisky mountain goat. We realized then that we had no chance of catching him.

It was at that very moment that there occurred a most strange thing. We were just turning to go back to the Hall when there, on a small tor, outlined against the silver moon, I saw the silhouetted figure of a man, stood perfectly still. It was not the convict, for it was the wrong direction — and besides, I sensed this figure to be taller and slimmer. With a cry of surprise I pointed him out to the baronet, but by the time he had turned to look the man was obscured by clouds; and when the clouds had skudded past the figure had completely disappeared.

I explained what I had seen to Sir Henry.

"A warder from Princetown," he suggested reasonably, "out looking for Selden."

I wasn't so sure as my friend, but as we could do nothing more we set off for the Hall. As we walked I found that even I, whose greatest asset is common sense, began to wonder if there was indeed some mysterious and devilish creature out haunting those moody moors.

6 Death on the Moor

After breakfast Barrymore asked if he might speak freely on the matter of his brother-in-law.

"Of course, Barrymore," replied Sir Henry. 'What's on your mind?"

"I was very much surprised, sir, when I found out that you two gentlemen had been chasing Selden. The poor fellow has enough to fight against without me putting more on his track."

"If you had told us the secret of your own free will it would have been a very different matter," responded the baronet, somewhat tersely. "You only told us, or rather your wife only told us, when it was forced from you."

"I didn't think you would take advantage of it, Sir Henry."

"The man's a public danger, Barrymore. There are lonely houses scattered across these moors; Mr Stapleton's house, for example, with no-one but himself to defend it. There's no safety for anyone until he's back under lock and key."

"He'll break into no house, sir, I give you my solemn word on that. Nor will he trouble anyone at all in this county again. In two days or less the necessary arrangements will have been made and he will be on his way to South America from Plymouth. For pity's sake, Sir Henry, I beg you not to let the police know he's still on the moor. They've given up the chase there, and he can lie quiet until his ship is ready. You can't tell on him without getting me and my wife into trouble. I beg you, sir, to say nothing."

"Hmm. What do you say, Watson?"

I shrugged my shoulders and smiled. "If he were safely out of the country it would relieve the taxpayer of another burden."

"That's very true, doctor, very true. All right, Barrymore, you —"

"God bless you, sir, and thank you from my heart. It would have killed my poor wife if he'd been taken again."

"All right, Barrymore. You may go."

The butler vanished to the kitchens, after thanking us both many times. Like Sir Henry, I realized we were abetting a crime — but, like him, I felt we could do little else in the circumstances.

I retired to the library with my coffee to write my latest epistle to Holmes — a long one, this, recounting the strange events of the night — and in the afternoon I walked to Combe Tracey to catch the last post.

On my way back I was passing Lafter Hall when I was hailed from an upstairs window by Mr Frankland, the eccentric old man who lived there alone. I had met him briefly two days before, when calling on Dr Mortimer.

"Good day to you, Dr Watson!" he called out with good humour. "Come upstairs to have a

glass of wine and congratulate me!"

I went into the house and climbed to his room, a small chamber dominated by a telescope mounted on a tripod by the window.

"Have you ever wondered how this convict killer gets his food without being caught, Dr Watson?" he asked, stooping over his telescope.

"Yes, yes. I have," I replied. "It's a real mystery."

"Oh no it isn't. I've seen his messenger with my own eyes — through this telescope. It's a boy, and I've seen him take food and other things up to the moor these past two days, around this time as a matter of fact."

Selden wouldn't need two sources of food, nor risk them. So there was someone else hiding out on the moor — and this old man had stumbled across his supply line.

"How can you be sure the boy is aiding the criminal?"

"You may be very sure, sir," he answered, "that I have good grounds before coming to such an opinion. I've seen the boy three times with his bundle, twice in the afternoon and once in the morning. I've been able — but wait a moment, Dr Watson. Do my eyes deceive me, or is that him?"

It was several miles off, but I could make out a small dark dot against the dull green hillside.

"Come, sir, come!" cried Frankland, pulling me towards the telescope. "See for yourself! Quick, before he disappears."

Sure enough there he was — a small urchin with a bundle over his shoulder, toiling up the hill towards the tor. When he reached the top he paused for a moment, looked all around him, and then vanished over the crest of the hill.

"Well, am I right?"

"Certainly — there's a boy who seems to have some secret errand."

"And what the errand is even a county constable could guess," said Frankland. "But not one word shall those people have from me, Dr Watson, and I bind you to secrecy too. Not a word — do you understand?"

I was only too willing to keep his secret, whatever his reasons may have been. I assured him that his secret was safe with me and, resisting all temptations to stay and finish the decanter of wine, I set off. Once out of sight of Lafter Hall I veered across the edge of the moor to the top of the hill where I had seen the boy. He was nowhere to be seen, but below me there were two stone huts, the farther of them in a reasonable condition. This must be the burrow where the stranger lurked, I thought, for there was even a vague pathway leading to it.

My nerves tingled as I approached the hut; I tossed aside my cigarette and burst through the blanket that acted as a rough door. But the place was empty.

There were ample signs that someone had lived there for several days, but there was no clue as to his identity. So, as the late afternoon gave way to evening, I sat and waited for the return of this strange home's lodger.

It was a good while — but then I heard him. Some distance away came the sharp clink of a boot striking a stone. Then another, and another, coming nearer and nearer. I grabbed a cudgel and shrank back against the wall by the door, determined not to reveal myself until I had a chance of seeing something of the stranger.

There was a long pause, showing that he had stopped. My heart beat faster and faster. Then

once more the footsteps approached and a long shadow fell across the opening of the hut.

"It's a lovely evening, my dear Watson," said a familiar voice. "I really think that you would be more comfortable outside than in."

For a few moments I stood breathless, hardly able to believe my ears. Then my senses and my voice came back to me, while a crushing weight of worry seemed to be lifted from my soul. That cold, incisive, ironic tone could belong to only one man in all the world.

"Holmes!" I cried, diving outside the hut and shaking him by the hand. "I was never more glad to see anyone in all my life!"

"Or more astonished, perhaps?" he replied, leading me back into the hut.

"Well, I must confess to it, yes."

"The surprise was not all on one side, Watson, I assure you. I had no idea that you had found my retreat, and still less that you were inside it, until I was within a dozen paces of the door."

"My footprint?" I asked.

"No, Watson. I fear that I could not recognize your footprint from any other in the world. If you really wish to deceive me you must change your tobacconist, for when I see the stub of a cigarette marked '*Bradley, Oxford Street,*

London', I know that my friend is in the neighbourhood."

He raised the stub for me to see it, and we both smiled. "Knowing your admirable tenacity, I was convinced you were waiting in ambush for the tenant to return. So you thought I was the criminal?"

"I didn't know what to expect, but I was determined to find out."

"Excellent, Watson! And how did you find me? You saw me last night, perhaps, when I was unwise enough to allow the moon to rise behind me for a few moments?"

"So that was you! Yes, I saw you then."

"And you have searched all the huts on the moor until you stumbled on this one?

"No. Your boy has been seen more than once, and that pointed me to where I should look."

"Hmm. Mr Frankland of Lafter Hall, no doubt. Well done, Watson."

"I'm glad from my heart that you are here. The responsibility and the mystery were both becoming too much for my nerves. But how in heaven's name did you come here — and what have you been doing? I thought you were in Baker Street!"

"That's what I wished you to think, my dear doctor."

"Then you use me but do not trust me," I said. "I think I've deserved better at your hands, Holmes."

"My dear fellow, you have been invaluable to me in this as in many other cases, and I beg that you will forgive me if I have seemed to play a little trick on you. In truth it was partly for your sake that I did it, and it was an appreciation of the danger that you were in that led me to come down so soon. My presence at the Hall would have put our formidable opponent on his guard; as it is, I have remained a roaming, unknown factor, ready to throw in my weight at the critical time."

"But why keep me in the dark, as well as Sir Henry?"

"For you to know would not have helped us, and may possibly have led to my discovery. An unnecessary risk would have been run."

I was still dwelling on the deception that had been practised on me when my thoughts were shattered by a terrible screaming sound, as a prolonged yell of anguish burst out from somewhere far off across the shadowy plain.

Holmes sprung to his feet, and peered out into the gathering night. Now it burst upon our ears, nearer, louder, more urgent than before.

"Where is it?" whispered Holmes. And I knew from the thrill of his voice that he, the man of iron, was shaken to the very soul. "Where is it, Watson?"

I pointed into the darkness. "Over there, I think!"

"No, there, surely!"

Again the agonized cry swept through the silent night, nearer than ever; and a new sound mingled with it, a deep, rumble, musical yet menacing, rising and falling like the murmur of the sea.

"The hound!" cried Holmes, suddenly taking off from the hut. "Come, Watson, come — and pray to God we're not too late!"

He started running over the moors, and I followed at his heels. Then, from somewhere among the broken ground immediately in front of us, there came a despairing yell and then a dull, heavy thud. We stopped and listened — but no other sound now broke the heavy silence of the windless night.

Blindly we ran through the gloom, blundering against boulders, panting up hills and rushing down slopes, at every rise eagerly looking about us. But there was no sign. Then a low moan fell on our ears. There it was again, on our left!

On that side a ridge of rocks ended in a steep cliff, which overlooked a stone-strewn slope. On its face was spread-eagled some irregular shaped object — and as we ran towards it the shape hardened into that of a man, face down, prostrate on the ground. As we climbed down the slope towards it I turned sick and faint; for the body was none other than that of Sir Henry Baskerville!

"The brute! The brute!" I shouted. "Oh, Holmes, I shall never forgive myself for having left him to his ghastly fate!"

Holmes stooped over the body. "I would be far more to blame than you, Watson — if it were true — for in order to have my case well rounded off and complete I would have thrown away the very life of my client. But do not upset yourself, my dear fellow. Look here — the man has a beard!"

I took a look for myself. "It's not Sir Henry. It's Selden, the convict."

Then, amid my unbridled relief, all became clear to me — and then to my companion. I told Holmes about how Sir Henry had consoled Barrymore by presenting him with part of his wardrobe; the butler must have handed it on to Selden to help him in his planned escape from the country.

"Then the clothes have been the cause of this poor fellow's death," said Holmes. "It's clear enough that the hound was given the scent by some article of clothing of Sir Henry's — and when let loose ran this poor creature down by mistake. The immediate question is — what do we do with the body? We cannot leave it here to the foxes and the ravens."

Before I could reply I noticed a figure approaching us across the moor, and I quickly recognized the jaunty walk of the naturalist.

"Why, Dr Watson," said he as he came up to us, "you're the last person I expected to see out on the moor at this time of the evening. Dear me, what's this? It's not — don't tell me it's our friend Sir Henry?"

He hurried past us and stooped over the dead man. I heard a sharp intake of breath.

"Who — who's this?" he asked.

"It's Selden, the escaped convict from Princetown."

Stapleton rose, looking sharply from Holmes to me. "Dear me! What a dreadful affair. How did he die?"

"It seems he broke his neck by falling down these rocks. My friend and I were strolling out on the moor when we heard a cry."

"Yes, I heard a cry too. Tell me, did you — did you hear anything else besides a cry?"

"No," said Holmes. "Did you?"

"No."

"In that case, what exactly do you mean?"

"Oh, you know the stories that the peasants tell about a phantom hound and so on. It's said to be heard at night out on the moor. I was simply wondering if there was any evidence of such a hound tonight."

"We heard nothing of the kind, I'm glad to say," I lied.

"And what is your theory about this poor fellow's death, Dr Watson?"

"I've no doubt that anxiety and exposure drove him off his head. He has rushed round the moor in a crazed state until he finally fell over this cliff in the dark and broke his neck."

"That does seem the most resonable explanation, I suppose. What do you think about it, Mr Holmes?"

My friend bowed his compliments. "You are quick at identification," he said coolly.

"We've been expecting you in these parts ever since Dr Watson came down. It's unfortunate you were met by a tragedy."

"Yes, indeed. But I think my colleague's explanation covers the facts. I'm sorry that I shall take only an unpleasant memory of the moor back to London with me tomorrow."

"Oh, you return tomorrow?" asked Stapleton unnecessarily. "I hope your visit has cast at least some light upon the things that have puzzled us?"

Holmes shrugged his shoulders. "One cannot always have the success for which one hopes. An investigator needs facts, not legends or rumours. It has not been a satisfactory case."

Stapleton looked hard at Holmes, then at me. "I would suggest carrying this poor fellow to my house, but I'm afraid that it would give my sister such a fright that I would rather do otherwise. I think if we put something over him the body will be safe until morning."

And so it was agreed. Resisting Stapleton's offer of hospitality, Holmes and I set off for Baskerville Hall, leaving the naturalist to return home alone.

"What a nerve the fellow has!" whispered Holmes when we were well away from the scene. "How he pulled himself together in the face of what must have been a paralyzing shock when he found that the wrong man had fallen victim to his evil plot. How casually he put his questions about what we had heard and what our theories are! I told you in London, Watson, when he was unknown to us, and will tell you again now — we have never had a foe more worthy of our steel."

"It is he, then, who dogged us in London?"

"So I deduce."

"And the warning — who did that come from?"

"His wife. The lady who passes here as Miss Stapleton is really his wife, not his sister."

"Good heavens! But why the elaborate deception?"

"Because he saw that she would be very much more use to him in the character of a free woman."

"Are you sure of all this, Holmes?"

"Quite, Watson. There is no one easier to trace than a schoolmaster. A little investigation showed me that a school up north had come to grief under dire circumstances, and that the man who had owned it — the name was different — had disappeared with his wife. The description agreed, and when I later learned that the missing man was devoted to insects and so on — indeed a great authority on butterflies — the identification was complete."

All my unspoken instincts, my vague suspicions, suddenly took shape and centred on this naturalist. In that colourless man, with his straw hat and butterfly net, I saw something terrible — a creature of infinite patience and craft, with a smiling face and a murderous heart.

"What a pity he's seen you here."

"Yes, it is, Watson. But there's no getting out of it."

"Do you think he will change his plans, now that he knows you're here?"

"It may cause him to be more cautious; or it may drive him to desperate measures at once. Like most clever criminals, he may be too confident in his own cleverness, and imagine that he has completely deceived us."

"Why shouldn't we simply arrest him now?"

"My dear Watson, you were born to be a man of action. Your instinct is always to do something energetic. But supposing that we had him arrested tonight — what would that accomplish? We could prove nothing against him. There's the devilish cunning of it."

"Surely we have some kind of case?"

"Not a shadow of one — only theory and conjecture. We should be laughed out of court if we came with a story and such thin evidence. In the case of both Sir Charles and Selden there is no direct connection between the hound and the man's death. No-one has ever seen it. We heard it, but we couldn't prove it was running on the convict's trail. And there's the complete absence of motive. No, my dear fellow. We must accept the fact that we have no case at present — and that we may have to run some risks in order to establish one."

I asked him how he proposed to do that, but by then Holmes was lost in thought and I could draw nothing more from him until we reached the gates of Baskerville Hall.

"Are you staying here tonight?" I asked.

"Yes — I can see no reason for further concealment. But one last word, Watson. Say nothing of the hound to Sir Henry. Let him think that Selden's death was as Stapleton would have us believe. He will then have a better nerve for the ordeal he will have to endure tomorrow when, if I remember correctly, you are to dine with these people. And now, if we are too late for dinner, I think that we are both ready for our suppers."

7   Fixing the Nets

Sir Henry was more pleased than surprised to see Holmes, for he had for some time been expecting him down from London. He did raise his eyebrows, however, when he found that my friend had neither luggage nor an explanation for its absence.

My first task was the unpleasant one of breaking the news of Selden's death to Barrymore and his wife, both of whom seemed to be more relieved than grieved by the affair. Then, after a belated supper, we explained to the baronet as much of our experiences as we thought he should know.

"But how about the case itself?" he asked. "Have you made anything out of the tangle? I don't know that Watson and I are that much the wiser since we came down."

"I think I shall be in a position to make the situation rather clearer to you before very long, Sir Henry. It has been a difficult, complicated business, and there are several points on which we still want light. But it is coming, all the same. What I require now is complete co-operation and trust from you."

"I will try to do whatever you tell me."

"Good — and I must ask you to do it blindly, without asking the reason."

"Just as you like."

"If you will do this I think the chances are that our little problem will be solved."

And with that he rose from his chair and promptly retired to his bed.

I was up early in the morning, but Holmes was afoot earlier still, for as I dressed I saw him coming up the drive.

"Yes, we should have a full day today," he remarked when we met downstairs, rubbing his hands together with gleeful anticipation. "The nets are all in place, and the drag is about to begin. We'll know before the day is out whether we have caught our lean-jawed pike or whether he has got through the meshes."

"Have you been out on the moor already?"

"No, Watson. I have sent a wire to Inspector Lestrade in London asking for his presence here and a warrant for our friend's arrest; and I have sent a report to Princetown Prison on the death of Selden. They will take care of the body, and I can promise that nobody here will be further troubled by the matter. Oh yes, and I have communicated with my faithful boy messenger, who seemed quite upset that I must finish with his admirable services."

"So, what's the next move?"

"To see Sir Henry. Ah, here he is."

"Good morning, gentlemen. I must say, Mr Holmes, you look like a general who's planning a battle with his chief of staff."

"That is the exact situation. Watson was asking for orders."

"And so do I."

"Very good. You are engaged, as I understand, to dine with our friends the Stapletons tonight."

"I hope that you will come also. They're very hospitable people, and I'm sure that they would be very glad to see you."

"I fear that Watson and I must go to London."

"To London?"

"Yes, I think that we should be more useful there at the present time."

The baronet's face lengthened. "I hoped that you were going to see me through this business, Mr Holmes. The Hall and the moor are not very pleasant places when you're alone."

"My dear fellow, you must trust me implicitly and do precisely what I ask, as we agreed last night. You can tell your friends that we should have been happy to have come with you, but that urgent business required us to be in town. We hope to return to Devonshire very soon. Will you remember to give them that message?"

"If you insist on it."

"There is no alternative, I assure you."

I saw by the baronet's knotted brow that he was deeply hurt by what he regarded as our desertion.

"When do you wish to go?" he asked coldly.

"Immediately after breakfast. We will drive in to Combe Tracey, but Watson will leave his things here as a pledge that he will come back to you. Watson, you will send a note to Stapleton to tell him that you regret that you cannot come tonight."

"I've a good mind to go to London with you," said the baronet. "Why should I stay here alone?"

"First, because it is your duty. Second, because you gave me your word that you would do as you were told. Now, one more direction. I wish you to drive to Merripit House this evening. Send back your trap, however, and let them know that you intend to walk home."

"To walk across the moor?"

"Yes."

"But that's the very thing which you have always warned me never to do."

"This time you may do it with safety, Sir Henry, I assure you. If I had not every confidence in your nerve and courage I would not suggest it, but it is essential that you should do it."

"Then I'll do it."

"And as you value your life, do not go across the moor in any direction save along the straight path which leads from Merripit House to the Grimpen Road, and is your natural way home."

"I'll do just as you say."

"Very good. I should be glad to get away as soon after breakfast as possible, so as to reach London in the afternoon."

We had finished breakfast and were just about to leave when we had a visitor at Baskerville Hall — a somewhat unexpected one in the circumstances. It was none other than Stapleton, come to check on the situation with Selden's body and to remind Sir Henry of their engagement that evening. The baronet said he would be there, but we both declined the offer, stating that we were about to return to London on urgent business.

And so we left Baskerville Hall and headed for Combe Tracey. Holmes was in fine form in the carriage, having seen his plan take shape.

"Watson," he said eagerly. "that chance visit just now has provided us with the missing link! Not only did it afford the chance to further convince our foe that we are indeed off to London — but when he stood in the dining-hall you could not fail to see it — he was almost a reflection of the portrait behind him, the very reincarnation of Sir Hugo. The man is a Baskerville, my dear doctor, and no mistake."

"With obvious designs on the title, no doubt!"

"Exactly, Watson! That was the final proof I needed — the motive for killing Sir Charles and trying to kill Sir Henry. We have him, Watson, we have him; and I dare swear that before the night is out he will be fluttering in our net as helpless as one of his own butterflies. A pin, a cork, and a card — and we add him to the Baker Street collection!"

At the post office Holmes sent a message to one of his contacts in London, who was to send a wire to Sir Henry Baskerville just after the scheduled arrival of the next train from Devon at Paddington. This would say that if the baronet finds the pocket-book Holmes left at the Hall he is to send it by registered post to Baker Street. This would convince Sir Henry of our absence and, if mentioned by the baronet, also reassure Stapleton that we were indeed far away.

At the station there was a message for Holmes, just in from London: 'Wire received. Coming down with unsigned warrant. Arrive 5.45. Lestrade.'

Holmes' plan was starting to unfold. He would use Sir Henry to convince Stapleton that we had really gone, when all the time we would be right on the spot. Already I seemed to see our nets drawing close round our catch, and felt a tingle at the prospect of landing him.

8 The Hound of the Baskervilles

We made ourselves as scarce as possible during the long wait for the train, for it was not impossible that Stapleton should be checking on us, either himself or through a third party.

When the train finally arrived, on time, Lestrade was indeed on it, and the three of us shook hands.

"It had better be pretty good to bring me all this way, Holmes," said the Inspector with only a trace of a smile.

"The biggest thing for years," replied Holmes in whispered tones. "But we have hours before we need start. I think we may employ it by getting some refreshment, and I will fill you in on some of the detail. Then, Lestrade, we will take the London fog out of your throat by giving you a breath of the pure night-air of Dartmoor. Have you ever been here? No, I thought not. Well, I think I can promise you that you will not easily forget your first visit."

In the corner of the local tea-rooms, Holmes put Lestrade in the picture about the circumstances

of the case. The detective listened intently, almost reverentially — a far cry from the scorn he had showed for my companion when they had first met some years before.

"Tell me, Holmes," I said when he had finished. "How much of this did you know when you left London?"

"I knew little for certain, but suspected a lot. My enquiries showed that Roger Baskerville, who fled to South America and was thought to have died childless, in fact had a son. Having illegally secured a good sum of money in Costa Rica, and leaving his wife behind, he returned to England under the name of Vandeleur and set up a school in Yorkshire. Because of deaths from an epidemic he was forced to sell the ailing school and, changing his name to Stapleton, bought Merripit House with the last of his money.

"I believe his plans were hazy when he came here, but that he meant mischief is shown by the fact that from the start he took his wife with him as his sister. He cultivated a friendship with Sir Charles and with Dr Mortimer, from whom he learned that the baronet's heart was weak — and that he was about to go to London for treatment.

"His ingenious mind suggested a way in which Sir Charles could be done to death, and yet it would be virtually impossible to bring home the guilt to the real murderer.

"All my suspicions were confirmed here — first by his presence near the body of Selden so soon after his death, and then finally, if it were needed, by the likeness in the portrait. The rest you both know."

"The problem for me, Holmes, is that I cannot arrest someone for being related to a dead man," said Lestrade. "I must have proof."

"Exactly so, Inspector. That's why I have exploited the situation tonight and constructed this elaborate set-up — that you may have the proof you need to put away this vicious criminal. Now, are you armed?"

"I have my revolver."

"Good. We, too, are ready."

It had already been dark some time when we left the tea-rooms and boarded the wagon hired by Holmes that afternoon. As we headed up towards the moor on our strange mission, and the cold wind blew on our faces, my nerves began to tingle with anticipation.

The wagon stopped a mile or so from Merripit

House, and we all stepped down. Holmes paid the driver off and we watched him turn round to return to Combe Tracey.

"You're mighty close about this affair, Holmes," said Lestrade as we set off. "What's the game now?"

"A waiting game, Inspector. I must ask you to walk quietly — and not to talk."

We moved cautiously along the track as though bound for the house, but Holmes halted us when we were still some way from it.

"This will do," he whispered. "We shall make our little ambush here. You've been there, Watson — which is the dining-room?"

I explained the layout of the house and then he was off, creeping towards it. We could just make out his shape as he approached the latticed window. After some time he came running back to our position.

"There were only two men in the room — Sir Henry and Stapleton. As I watched the host left the room, while Sir Henry filled his glass again. I heard the crisp sound of boots on gravel, and looking over, saw the naturalist pause at the door of an outhouse. He was only a minute or so inside, then I heard him lock the door and return to the house."

"The lady is not there?" I asked.

"I could not see her, Watson."

Holmes explained that we could do little more than wait for our friend's departure, and track his course. With the air getting colder and damper, that wait seemed to last an age. Indeed

Lestrade and I began to wonder if Holmes' plan had gone seriously wrong — that Sir Henry might already be dead.

Then, after two hours or so, we all became aware of a very worrying development: the dense fog that hung over the Grimpen Mire was drifting slowly in our direction.

"It's moving towards us, Watson," said Holmes, more worried than I had ever seen him. "The one thing on earth that could have disarranged my plans. But he can't be long now; it's already well past ten. Our success, even his life, may depend on his leaving before the fog is over the path across the moor."

With every minute that passed, however, the white misty plain that covered half the moor was moving steadily closer. The first thin wisps of it were now curling across the golden square of the house's lighted window, and the far wall of the

orchard was already invisible. And, as we watched, the fog-wreaths came crawling round both corners of the house and rolled slowly into one dense bank, on which the upper floor and the roof floated like a strange ark on a shadowy sea.

"If he isn't out in ten minutes the path will be covered," said Holmes. "In twenty minutes we won't be able to see each other, let alone Sir Henry."

"Should we move back to higher ground?" I suggested.

"Yes, Watson, I think that would be as well."

As the fog-bank flowed onwards we fell back before it until we were half a mile or so from the house. And still the white sea swept slowly but surely on.

"We're going too far!" said Holmes, now almost with a tone of panic in his voice. "We

154

dare not take the chance of his being overtaken before he can reach us. At all costs we must hold our ground where we are!"

A few seconds later the sound of swift steps broke the eerie silence of the moor. Crouching among the stones, we stared intently at the silver-topped bank of fog in front of us. The steps grew louder, and through the fog, as through a curtain, there came the man we were awaiting. He passed close to where we hid, moving swiftly, glancing continually over his shoulder.

Then it happened. First, a long, low growl echoed out of the fog, now only yards away. I braced myself for what might emerge, and thought I was prepared; but even so I lurched back, my frozen hand grabbing pathetically for my pistol, my mind almost paralyzed by the dreadful shape that had sprung out at us from the white shadows.

A hound it was, an enormous thing, and not such a hound as any mortal eye has ever seen. Its huge body was a ghastly luminous blue, its eyes glowed with a smouldering glare, its muzzle and dewlap were defined in flickering flame. Never in the delirious dream of a disordered brain could anything more hellish or more frightening be conceived than that form and face which broke on us from the wall of fog.

The huge creature was leaping down the track with huge bounds, following hard on the steps of our friend. We were so stunned that it took us some time to recover our senses. Then we moved after it. Holmes, Lestrade and I all fired almost together and the beast gave a hideous howl; one of us at least had hit it. But it did not stop; still it pursued Sir Henry.

Far away on the path we saw our friend looking back as he ran, his face white with fright in the moonlight, his hands already raised in

156

horror, glaring in fear at his hunter.

But that yelp from the hound had blown all our fears to the winds; if he could be hurt then he was mortal, and if we could wound it we could kill it. We flew up the track, hearing scream after scream from Sir Henry and the constant deep roar of the hound. We all but lost each other in the fog, but I was in time to see the beast spring on its victim, knock him to the ground and worry at his throat.

"Mind Sir Henry if you shoot!" yelled the voice of Lestrade. But the next instant Holmes had emptied five barrels of his revolver into the creature's body. With a last howl of agony and a twist in the air it rolled on to its back, its feet pawing the air furiously, and then fell back on its belly across the limp figure of Sir Henry.

I stooped, still panting with fear, and pressed my pistol to its shimmering head. But it was useless to pull the trigger: the giant hound was dead.

Sir Henry lay insensible where he had fallen. We dragged the dog off him, then tore away his collar. I breathed a prayer of gratitude when I saw there was no sign of a serious wound. As I supported his weight our friend's eyelids began to flicker and he made a feeble effort to move. Lestrade thrust his brandy flask between the baronet's teeth, and in a few seconds two frightened eyes were looking up at us.

"My God," he whispered. "What was it? What in heaven's name was it?"

"It's dead, whatever it is," replied Holmes. "We've laid the family ghost once and for all."

In mere strength and size it was an awesome creature that lay near us. It was neither bloodhound nor mastiff, but a staggering combination of the two — gaunt, savage, half-starved, but still as large as a small lioness. Even now, in the stillness of death, the huge jaws seemed to be dripping with a bluish flame and the deep-set, cruel eyes were ringed with fire.

Holmes placed his hand on the head, and as he held up his finger it glowed in the darkness.

"Phosphorous?" I suggested.

"A cunning preparation of it," he replied.

"There's no smell which might have interfered with his power of scent. We owe you a deep apology, Sir Henry, for having exposed you to this. I was prepared for a large hound, but nothing like this — and the fog gave us little chance."

"You saved my life, Mr Holmes."

"Having first put it at great risk. Are you strong enough to stand?"

"Give me another shot of that brandy and I'll be ready for anything," replied the baronet bravely. "What do you intend to do now?"

"Lestrade and myself will head for the house; you and Watson will follow as quickly as you can. We have our case — now we want our man. It's a thousand to one he is at the house — the shots will have warned him and in any case he would have followed the track of the hound — but we must make sure."

Sir Henry and I managed almost to keep up with the others, and once inside the house I was able to make him comfortable and join them as they searched the rooms. No corner of the place was missed, but there was no sign of Stapleton. On the upper floor, however, one of the rooms was locked.

"There's someone in there!" cried Lestrade. "I can hear movement!"

A faint rustling and moaning came from within. Holmes struck the door just above the lock with the flat of his foot, and it flew open.

We were faced not by Stapleton but by his wife, tied to a bedpost and with a crude gag round her mouth, her eyes full of grief and shame. In a few seconds Lestrade had torn off the gag and unravelled her bonds, and Mrs Stapleton sank to the floor. As her beautiful head fell on her chest I saw the clear red weal of a whiplash across her neck.

"The brute!" I cried. "Lestrade, your brandy bottle, quickly!"

She took a sip from the flask and opened her eyes. "Is he safe?" she asked. "Did he escape?"

"He cannot escape us, madam," said Holmes.

"No, no, I didn't mean my husband. Sir Henry — is he safe?"

"Yes," I answered. "He's resting downstairs."

"Thank God! Thank God!" she said. "And the dreadful hound?"

"It is dead," said Holmes.

She gave a long sigh, then broke into a soft sob.

"Tell us where we can find him," said Holmes. "If you have ever aided him in evil, help us now and tell us where he is."

"There is but one place he could have fled," she replied. "There's an old tin mine on an island in the heart of the Grimpen Mire. It was there he kept his dog. That's where he would go."

"Do you think you could lead us to it?" asked Holmes.

"I'll try — I helped him to plant the guiding wands when we first arrived here. But it's a dangerous business."

"Watson, you look after Sir Henry. Lestrade and I will go after Stapleton."

The three of them were gone less than half an hour. They had only just reached the edge of the mire when they heard the unmistakable sound of a man yelling desperately for help — pleading for rescue from the treacherous bog. Mrs Stapleton knew it could mean only one thing: that her villainous husband had met his end in the very place that had been his own special, dark secret.

When, finally, the fog lifted and Sir Henry had made something of a recovery, we all made our way back to Baskerville Hall. The grim story of the Stapletons could no longer be kept from the baronet, but it did not dent his feelings for Beryl; indeed he seemed to think all the more of her, and it was obvious that, once the clouds of this ghastly affair had blown away, she might well be a permanent fixture in his life.

It was she who had sent the warning letter, just as she had warned Sir Henry (and mistakenly myself) out on the moor. Virtually imprisoned by Stapleton in his London hotel, it was the only way she could get a message to the new baronet once she suspected her husband of his murderous plans.

The next day was clear and bright, and despite the exhausting adventures of the previous night all five of us had trekked to the edge of the mire by ten o'clock. Mrs Stapleton guided us to a point where a small path started across the bog, and then Holmes, Lestrade and I carefully picked our way through the undulating mass of decaying vegetation between the various reeds and small branches put down by the naturalist and his wife.

We had gone some considerable distance when I saw something dark protruding from the slime, and with Holmes acting as my anchor I could just reach it. It proved to be a brown boot, with '*Meyers, Toronto*' printed on the inside.

"It belongs to Sir Henry, all right, Watson," said Holmes, studying my find.

"Thrown there by Stapleton last night."

"Exactly. He kept it in his hand after using it to set the hound on Sir Henry's track. He must have been still clutching the evidence when he fled, but at this point hurled it away. We know that he came at least this far in safety."

But more than that we were never destined to discover, though there was much to surmise. There was no chance of finding footsteps in the mire, for the rising mud oozed swiftly in on them, but as we at last reached firmer ground beyond the morass we all looked eagerly for them. But no sign of them ever met our eyes. If the earth told a true story, then Stapleton never reached that island of refuge towards which he struggled through the fog that night. Somewhere in the heart of the great Grimpen Mire, down in the foul slime which had sucked him in, this cruel man is for ever buried.